New Southern Harmonies

Four
Emerging
Fiction Writers

Holocene 1998

ISBN 1-891885-00-6
First edition, May 1998

Hub City editors, John Lane and Betsy Wakefield Teter
Cover/book design and photography Mark Olencki

> Mark Olencki has exhibited his photography in competitions and shows
> throughout the Southeast since 1972, and his photographs are included in the
> permanent collection of the State of South Carolina, the Spartanburg County
> Regional Museum, and the private collections of many businesses and
> individuals. He lives in Spartanburg's historic downtown Hampton Heights
> neighborhood with Diana and their son, Weston. Mark is president of Olencki
> Graphics, inc., a photo/graphics design firm in Spartanburg.

Shaped note graphics from the original *Southern Harmony and Musical
Companion* by William Walker, 1835, courtesy of the Spartanburg
Regional Museum
Special thanks to Greg and his staff at Java Jive Coffee House and Cafe
in historic downtown Spartanburg for their tasty scones, rich coffee,
and invitingly eclectic interiors
Printed & bound by Thomson-Shore, Inc. in Dexter, Michigan

Hub City Writers Project
Post Office Box 8421
Spartanburg, South Carolina 29305
(864) 577-9349 • fax (864) 577-0188 • www.hubcity.org

Contents

ROSA SHAND . . . 8
You Got to be Cut Sharp - 11
Density of Sunlight - 18
Briar Patch - 31

SCOTT GOULD . . . 42
Bases - 45
Sort of a Prophet - 56
Nothing Fazes the Autopilot - 67

DENO TRAKAS . . . 88
Eugene - 91
The Philosopher's Landlord - 104
Center of the Universe - 120

GEORGE SINGLETON . . . 128
Outlaw Head and Tail - 132
How I Became a City Planner,
   with a Minor in History - 146
I Could've Told You if You Hadn't Asked - 157

BIOGRAPHIES . . . 172

Preface

In the early part of the nineteenth century there was a preacher in Spartanburg, William "Singin' Billy" Walker, who came up with shaped notes—a method where everybody could learn to sing hymns without reading traditional musical notation. Each note corresponded to a geometric shape, and that corresponded to a sound. Groups could make pleasing sounds with little knowledge of music, and it revolutionized church singing. He published his song book, *Southern Harmony*, in 1835, and it went on to sell over one million copies, Spartanburg's all-time best seller.

Stories are a kind of music for a community. These twelve stories are gathered from four writers—Rosa Shand, Deno Trakas, Scott Gould, and George Singleton—who live in the Spartanburg and Greenville areas of upstate South Carolina. All four are introduced by fiction writers of national reputations who are well-acquainted with the full range of their work—Josephine Humphreys, Shelby Hearon, Bret Lott, and Fred Chappell. Each of the writers, plus the four who introduce them, offers a voice, a perspective, a well-shaped note. What this collection presents is a fiction version of "Singin' Billy's" book. These stories make new Southern harmonies.

New Southern Harmonies is the kind of book I've dreamed of doing through the Hub City Writers Project from the beginning. It's a book of home-grown literary sure-things. These fiction writers have published over a hundred stories between them in dozens of the country's best literary magazines, and no one in the South aware of fiction will be a stranger to their names. They have graced the pages of *The Georgia Review*, *Playboy*, *Virginia Quarterly Review*, *The Black Warrior Review*, *Nimrod*, *The Oxford American*, and many more of today's best magazines. Some of these stories have been included in *New Stories from the South*; some of the writers have read their work on National Public Radio; and all of them have been invited to read at colleges, universities, and literary societies. The fact that not one of them has yet to publish a collection of stories speaks much more about the sad state of commercial publishing than it does about their accomplished, consistent work over the past several decades.

Years ago a young girl sat in front of me at a South Carolina Governor's School for the Arts interview. She was hoping to be one of the thirty admitted to the program. She had written her stories for her portfolio about Iowa, a place she'd never been.

"Where are you from?" I asked her.

"Walhalla," she said shyly.

"And have you always lived in Walhalla?" the other interviewer asked.

"Uh huh," she said. "I've never been out of South Carolina."

"Why did you write about Iowa?" I asked. "Why didn't you write about Walhalla?"

"Walhalla?" she said. "Nothing happens in Walhalla."

I don't need to tell you what every good fiction writer knows: *Everything* happens in the Walhallas of the world. These four fiction writers learned these lessons early: Look close around you; plow in red clay or dark loam, whichever you're provided; dig deep; listen close; hunker down to the local, whether it's Africa, Spartanburg, Kingstree, or Greenwood.

—John Lane
The Hub City Writers Project

On Rosa Shand

by Josephine Humphreys

ALL FICTION TELLS OF ENDANGERED LIVES,
AND SO I SUPPOSE EVERY STORY MUST HAVE A
VILLAIN. BUT IN STRONG STORIES—LIKE THESE THREE
by Rosa Shand—the villain is nameless . . . disguised
. . . and very much at large. Shand's characters are in
peril and they know it, but they can't quite identify
and locate the danger except by metaphor. They call
it a desert. A dead feeling. A blindness. In other
words, the big danger is not a force in its own right
but an absence of force. It is the possibility that
nothing will grow: nothing will quicken or make itself
known.

   Is this a danger felt most sharply by young
women? Maybe so. The youngest of Shand's narra-

tors, the eleven-year-old in "You
Got to be Cut Sharp," is caught
in the keen pain of youthful
despair. Shamed by her artist-
mother's strangeness, she has
ironically made herself strange
as well, and she senses her
decline into isolation. "A bad
feeling began to get in me," she
says. (And there is surely no
better way to write that sentence.
Rosa Shand is a writer of arrest-
ing grace, but she also has an
ear for the blunt, plain phrase
that modulates, making for a
language both tough and supple.)
This is a story about the messiness of good things, of art
in particular and human charac-

ter in general; but the narrator's understanding of that lesson seems to come too late.

The slightly older girl (fourteen) who is the seeing character in "The Density of Sunlight" has a better chance of understanding, I think, not because she's older but because she is given a place. The daughter of Americans living in "the middle of Africa," Rachel is already connected to the world, so that when she becomes suddenly endangered—this time not by art but by passion—she is better able to steady herself. Yet the story clearly suggests something quite complicated: that deliverance may lie right at the heart of the danger, and that risks should be run, not dodged. Love is a mess. Shand reveals in one quick brilliant stroke Rachel's final decision—to acquiesce, choosing silence—but there can be no doubt it is her triumph.

I read "Briar Patch" as a story about the American South, and therefore a story about the messiness of history and our dire need for it. Here it is not the young woman who narrates or sees; she has become the story rather than the teller, and now it's her Yankee fiance who struggles to understand the perils she represents. He is about to marry into a "quicksand of a country," the very opposite of his own "real, decent, straightforward world where it's clean—where there's light, where things are clear and black and white . . ." Well, of course, he's right. The old place is suffocating under vines. The old lady who's going to be his in-law is "lying every syllable she speaks." But he starts to listen, and he starts to get interested.

Because this is exactly what Rosa Shand knows and wants us to know: A real, decent, straightforward world may not always be in our best interests, may not be quite enough to live on, and may not even exist. She is giving us, in these stories, a look at something more evocative and hazardous, burdened, spirited, difficult—and true.

—*Josephine Humphreys is the author of three novels, including* Dreams of Sleep, *winner of the PEN/Faulkner Award in 1984. She lives on Sullivan's Island in South Carolina.*

You Got to be Cut Sharp

I keep thinking of Betsy's house, like that must have been what made it all go bad in the first place. Because after that first time I went there I kept imagining her house and used to have something like nightmares about what would happen if Betsy ever came to mine. I guess after that everything got worse and worse and worse.

Betsy lived in one of those magazine houses with all the same whitish rugs everywhere you stepped, even in the corners, and no tubes of paint or books or papers lying around but just cleaned-up-looking glass tables with maybe a little pot of china flowers on them. Every one of her dining room chairs was just the same as the other ones and they all stood around the table like nobody ever sat in them. And there never were any clothes or dishes under the chairs or sofas or even under her bed. I know because I looked.

That day I was sitting on her sofa with nothing to do so I started feeling around under all the cushions and I didn't find one thing except some tag hooked on to the cushion like it was still in the store on sale. And then in her kitchen she poured me a drink—out of a kind of bare refrigerator with only a few little covered jars on the shelves, like even that place had been scrubbed out. And when a bit of this lemonade got spilled like it always does, Betsy went right over to the sink and grabbed a sponge and wiped that splash up off the floor like it was on a table. I started to ask her what she was doing that for but I saw she hadn't even thought about not doing it so I knew she wouldn't know what I was talking about.

I watched her getting things, and I noticed in that whole kitchen they didn't have one miscellaneous drawer that I could see—like we call all of ours. All those drawers were closed up tight with not one teaspoon sticking out. I guess you were expected to remember where everything was every time you wanted something because you certainly couldn't see in.

Another thing that made me feel funny—she had one of those fancy hotel kind of bathrooms with drawers and cabinets even under the basin, instead of pipes and rags. She opened up a drawer and there were shiny new-looking objects—fingernail clippers and all the hairpins in a box and a toothpaste tube with the top on it without even any droppings anywhere—a whole drawer without one trace of little brown bullets. You couldn't smell a thing and the toilet looked so white it might have come out of the dishwasher. I had a specially eerie feeling looking in the mirror—you could see everything all sharp and exact without one smudge. The outline of my face might have been cut out with a knife—there wasn't fuzzy room for secrets anywhere. It was frightening, like the feeling in an echoing steely-glass hospital with clipped white nurses clicking through. After a while I got scared I might have to use a towel or splash water in the basin or drop a crumb or something and they would know it was me. They would know I wasn't cut in that sharp way people had got to be cut if they wanted to fit. I just wanted to go home.

I had a dead feeling in that house. But still, I guess after that I began to think I saw why people looked funny when they came to my house. So I mostly stopped bringing people. I remember, before, I'd felt sorry for other kids when I saw how mean their mothers were, like always asking them if they'd hung up their coat or put their glasses in the sink.

But then a bad feeling began to get in me. My mother would be in the middle of one of her paintings. She'd be using the living room because there wasn't any other room, what with all the big paintings she was letting dry. One day I marched to the laundry pile on the dining room table to pull out some clothes to wear—see, our dining room and living room were all the same place—and her blue oil paint had gotten all over my pretty-new red corduroys. I never had even cared when it was all over my jeans and everything, but I was going to wear these pants to a party so I started crying and I screamed why couldn't she paint in her own room. She looked surprised and stopped painting and started moving things around and being sweet to me, promising me my pants would be all right. So I watched her pour turpentine all over those trousers and rub and rub until you couldn't even tell what color the pants were ever supposed to be anymore because the whole front of one leg was one big purple smudge. But there she was, being so good and trying so hard I couldn't stay mad and I decided all at once I wouldn't go to that party. She couldn't see anything wrong with those pants, at least not enough that anybody would notice, she said. And I was sad about the way I'd made her feel. I couldn't tell her I never would wear those pants again. I just went outside and walked around and didn't know what I would do, ever.

After that I started fighting to keep my clothes out of her way and she would even try to get paint off them when she noticed. It sounds crazy but one time when I hadn't even said one thing I saw her working away under the lamp in her room, trying and trying to get orange paint out of my white blouse. I just started crying quietly to my- self I was so glad she was my mama. I knew she'd never even seen paint on my clothes before.

But this new way of starting to care what things looked like was growing in me, and I got to feeling guilty. I knew she really did believe that nobody noticed what anything looked like. I think she was the only person in the world who took it completely for certain that all that ever ever matters is inside a person. Somebody like that is so out of place that they make everybody else feel weird, and I guess what I've started thinking now is that everything gangs up to make a person like that die. I was the first to gang up to make my mother die.

Maybe she did know other people didn't believe in just pure spirit like she did. Because when I was little, when my daddy was still here, I think I remember her throwing everything in closets if she knew he was coming. But when he went away she didn't have to do that anymore, and maybe she thought it was better just to live with me because I was only a child and I could learn to think about only what was important. With me, she could leave things like she needed them and could go on and paint humongous boards with dots and circles that nobody in the world would understand or buy. She could keep on and on and on. Maybe she thought somebody someday somewhere would get what she had in mind, or maybe she thought I would. I'm glad she couldn't know what would happen to those painted boards, how the red-nosed man next door built a doghouse out of them because nobody could figure out what else to do with them.

Maybe I really was my mama's only hope. And never mind, never mind anything, something just drove me to make everything get worse and worse. Like one time at my house I tried to give a girl some juice. I had to go find some glasses, and this girl followed me in my mother's room where I had to look under the bed. The girl wanted to know where my mother slept because there on top of the crumpled sheets was junk that you could tell had been there months and months. She

couldn't believe my mother just either slept on
that junk or pushed that pile over to one side. I
had never really thought about it before because
I guess I did the same thing. I had gotten used to
waking up in the middle of the night when I heard
a bump or a crash or a rolling noise across the
floor. It had even been nice-sounding because of
never getting scared of thieves or anything like
that. I would just know something had fallen off
my mama's bed when she humped around in her
sleep. But after that girl's visit, I got waked up one
night by one of those loud bangs—this time the
alarm clock bounced and clanged and jangled—
and I just lay there getting so mad I couldn't go
back to sleep. I couldn't get up then, but the next
morning when my mother came to cuddle in my
bed like she always did when she waked me up,
when she grinned and snuggled her nose all
around in my cheek, I flopped my face on the
other side and grunted. She always fixed me a
great big breakfast every morning, but that morning when I had to go find the salt and pepper in
her bed I got so wild when I looked at it I took
hold of her green-black sheet and yanked and
everything, even half a cup of coffee in my great-
grandmother's antique cup, came crashing down
under the paints and books and clothes and blan-
kets and the paper junk and dirty underpants.
Mama came running with a spoon in her hand like
I must have fainted or something and I just glared
at her and said I didn't care what I broke because
beds weren't supposed to be pig slops.

After that I turned twelve and I got genuinely
mean, no matter how bad I felt about everything
that was changing. She would still try to laugh
and cuddle and tease me out of my school-teacher
neatness, and of course sometimes I'd forget and
we'd be kind of happy together. But then I'd get a
sick feeling when I knew somebody might come
visiting and there wasn't anything I could do
about anything. One day I cried and slammed my
door and called her the laziest person in the uni-

verse—when even then I knew that wasn't what I meant because she had to go out and teach art to little kids at school all day long since Daddy died and she had to do everything else men usually do—except having all those screaming kids throwing clay around all day is a lot harder work than men ever have to do and she had something wrong with her blood anyway and that meant sometimes she fainted. I knew how she did all that and then stayed up way late at night because she felt like she couldn't live unless she got some of her own painting done too, no matter what people said about it. So it wasn't lazy that I meant to say. She just couldn't believe it was right to care about little things instead of the important things, and then she had to have me and all I did was get meaner and meaner, and so the one person she loved was getting to be just one big hate.

And that's what happened. I got to be one big sullen hate. She tried to do things differently, but really she never even saw most of the things that made me mad. Once in a while she still tried to tease and cuddle me about it all, but her eyes got sadder and sadder, and we said littler and littler. We both got edgier and edgier, and I would dream about how she used to hug and bite and laugh and how everything was so much happier in my home than in anybody else's home—in those days when I used to feel sorry for other children because their mamas weren't my mama. But even when I wanted her to cuddle me, something mean in me just ate me up, and so she never could, and that was all there was. The thing in her blood got worse and worse and one day when they took her to the hospital straight from school she never did come back.

I have to live with my grandmother now. My daddy's mama. I have one spot of my own. It's in my closet, where I have piles of Mama's things. Even the psychiatrist won't let my grandmother touch me in my closet. And so, when it's completely dark, when nobody in the world can see, when nobody can be jealous and nobody can set up traps to make me think I have to put my mind on what everything looks like, like other people do—when, then, I've wriggled down to sleep in paint-soaked rags and mama-smells just like I'm sinking in a great warm lake—then, in the dark, my mama tiptoes in and grins and snuggles down and rubs her nose all in my cheek and bites my ear and teases me and cuddles me and wiggles tight, all cozy tight in the black black dark, and makes it so we never have, ever ever ever, to look at any little thing, any tiny unimportant thing, again. Never and never and never.

The Density of Sunlight

There was always sunshine. Once when she was younger and somebody argued that there couldn't always have been sunshine because the place was dark with vines and overhanging fronds and dripped with mangoes and bananas then she had to say it rained. Maybe everyday in the wet season. But the greyness hadn't time to settle in before the sun came showering down on every-thing again and so it wasn't rain that she remem-bered. Not before Piers.

She lived in the semi-jungle, at what used to be a mission station called Mukono. Now it was two schools with all the hanger-on buildings that collected because everybody had to live on the place, in the mud-brick, tin-roofed structures dotted in the green between the mango and acacia and the jacaranda trees.

Her father taught history. He had yellow spurts of sideburns—which was where she, Rachel, got her long blond hair that little children here were always reaching up to touch, gently, tentatively, with a soft low crooning sound she had to get used to.

Her father was the one who was always sorting out the country and Kampala—they were all the time in Kampala for something—explaining why it was the Sikhs who did the building and the Patels who ran the printers and the Ismailis who started the high school and why the Baganda were so polite and the Acholi seemed so gruff and why the

Banyankole women were so fat but strode around like queens. Sometimes he explained a bit too much about all the intrigues of tribal politics— while her mother lounged in the sun and read novels. Or, if they had managed to dig up some literary man for their Entebbe picnics, her mother might break out of her spacey air of being completely out of everything and flail her arms around about some book she'd discovered. Her mother never cared about how the Kabaka's second wife had cut out the ssekibobo's daughter and she, Rachel, always felt sorry for her father when her mother gave up even pretending to listen to one of his interminable stories about whose mother's brother was connected with whom (those things were important, he said, if you were going to understand anything about the country's politics). Rachel thought he ought to tell those things just to her instead of bothering her mother but he never seemed to catch on. He kept trying to get her mother's attention, and it was like chugging and chugging at a motor that never had a chance of turning over.

The steady sunshine could sometimes be boring in Africa. One excitement—or something Rachel hoped would be excitement—was when a new teacher came, because the teachers came from everywhere. Beside the Africans there were English and Americans and Canadians and Irish and Germans, and even one man from India. Everybody at the school who had a car would drive the fifty miles to Entebbe (the airport) any day to see a new face. They would climb up on the sun-hot roof and lean over the rail and bet on who could pick out the new person first.

You could always tell about new people at a glance—even across a mile of glaring tarmac runway. You could count on a scrawny balding man with glasses or some English family with a fat little boy with no chin. But just when she had given up, just when she felt crushed under the jungle tombstone dropping on her at age fourteen, the next-door school pulled out a Piers. And she wasn't even at Entebbe when his plane dove in low over Lake Victoria and set him down in the sunshine.

She saw him Sunday after evensong. Already he seemed to be old friends with her mother and with, it looked like, all the women on the hill. He was outside the chapel in the middle of the splashy-flowered dresses (her mother was of course the different one in her bright red blouse and tight wrap-around skirt). Anybody would have had to stare at this man: His black eyes flamed like coals even if he did wear glasses, and even if his hair was straight and dark. He seemed louder than most Englishmen but that might have been because he spurted electric-quick funny asides. She could see him mimic people out of the corner of his mouth and already she could see it wasn't really mean because his jetty eyes would be laughing in the eyes of the person he was mocking—as if the one he were half mimicking (her mother, say) were the main one he was talking to.

That first time she stopped at the edge of his circle. When he saw her he dropped his antics. He twisted around to look at her and grinned "Hello" and his black eyes burned in her. He told her later he had caught himself from calling out "Hello my little beauty" because he had gotten confused and thought maybe she wasn't so little after all.

Almost always her mother had somebody to supper after Sunday evensong, mostly the single men around the hill—and now Piers was coming. And they were all walking up the path toward the house.

Those walks up the mountain path with Sunday company were like hanging in time because the air was very light and somehow fragile just that time of day. There was a goldish glow around the edge of things, the cricket whir was almost dizzying and you could smell the woodfire smoke around the hill. One thing about living on the

equator was that you could count on the sun
doing the same thing at the same time every day
all the year long and so those Sunday evenings on
the mountain path—in heady-gold and woodfire
air—got fixed forever in her mind.

It was Piers that night who stopped dead still
on the steepest part of the path, beside the line of
cassia trees. (The black hills all at once had
seemed to catch on fire around their rim.) His
hands were jammed in his pockets. He tossed
back his flopping streaks of hair the way he always
did and sort of fiercely whispered, "Nobody told
me the middle of Africa was this."

She loved him that instant, completely.

Piers taught English. He loved everything and he
could do everything, like playing any instrument he
touched. Once not long after he had come she heard
him playing on the chapel piano. She sat outside to
listen, fiddling with the drum sticks under the tiny
thatched-roof hut where they kept the biggest drum
in the country, the one they boomed when it was
time for services.

The piano stopped. He came out from the
shadow of the chapel, his whole face squinting
from his grin and from the drenching sunlight. He
started teasing her—a stupid thing about her
getting the prize for the quietest drum-playing he
had ever heard. (She made some witty reply like a
giggle.) And then it was just the two of them in
the little shed and he decided they would learn to
play the drums—as absolutely silently as she had
played—on, of course, the biggest drum in the
country. So he would tap and then he'd wait for
her to take the rhythm that he'd started. He
helped her along by holding his hands over hers
on the sticks—which made her face so searing hot
that she went rigid praying he wouldn't look at her
and guess. But soon—like always with him—they
were doubled over laughing because of course the
drumming wasn't quiet and black faces were
popping up from nowhere all around them.

Ezekiel, in his sticky yellow nylon shirt—one of
the students—decided he would show them how
the drums were really played and boomed loose
with a quick and counter-pointed complex pounding. She could see that Piers was nervous then.
He didn't want to stop Ezekiel—after all Piers had
started it all himself and Ezekiel was way-gone
into it, sweating, his eyes closed—while everybody
was dropping their work and rushing up like some
emergency.

They got stopped pretty soon but Piers made
weeks of jokes of it. Anytime the drums rolled he
would specially come whisper in her ear how it
was he and she who got things going on this hill.
But scariest of all to her was the way he put their
names together—as if they were meant to be that
way.

Then the plays started. Piers was putting on
the "Second Shepherd's Play" over at his school
and one afternoon he came to her house looking
for costumes. Her mother rummaged in the
trunks but mostly what she came up with were
filmy curtains. That would do. Piers took his shirt
off to get the idea. Across his chest with its mass
of black hair—deep-tanned now the muscles of
his shoulders were, from Uganda sunshine—her
mother slowly draped a long white flimsy thing.
Carefully she tied it on his shoulder like a toga.
She kept standing back to cock her head and
coming up to adjust and pat it while he stood
suspiciously eyeing her, purposely holding himself
ridiculously stiff like a patriarchal chief.

They went out to the "pine grove" next to the
house, the one her mother was so proud of because she'd had the trees planted when they had
come to Africa before she, Rachel, was born and
now the trees were a grove they could sit in. The
pines were just above a bank, a spot a little like
the one where Piers would put the play on at his
school so he was trying to get the effect—popping
up from behind the evergreens with his chest way
out, planting his stick down like a shepherd's staff

and booming out: "What the devil is this? He has a long snout!"

Children and garden boys came gawking. Piers and her mother (who put on plays at their college sometimes too) started interrupting each other with flashes of ideas about how the drums should sound and how somebody ought to come running in from the audience and how they'd get a little goat that looked just like a sheep. They laughed so crazily they leaned all over each other so after a while she, Rachel, just sat cross-legged in the thick grass at the edge of the grove watching the little game the birds were playing: wagtails bobbing up in the sunlight until they'd get too close to people and hop away from all the noise and then bob slowly back again. Suddenly Piers dropped next to her. His chest was naked under the gauze. His knee was touching hers and he looked at her with the fiercely penetrating look he got—serious, not joking—and asked her what it was that made people laugh. Just like that, as if she were a philosopher. As if it were the most important thing in all the world to him to know what she, a fourteen-year-old, thought about the subject. And the funny thing was that she came up with something he thought was brilliant—she didn't remember what now. She often did come up with those things when he asked that way— maybe because he thought she could. It was as if he had the power to create her.

But she see-sawed with him between that way of being about twenty, or still ten. Sometimes she was such a quivering mass that instead of thinking up answers when he talked she cried. And she couldn't even say why she was crying. He was awed—she could see that—the couple of humiliating times it happened. But one time he started to tease her about those tears like he teased her about everything. Then he dropped it, square in the middle, with his mouth hanging open. As if he knew he would never climb back out of that. He stared at her strangely—for such a long time that

when he finally looked away she couldn't hear
what anyone was saying.

Once he came to her house when her mother
wasn't there (she could see he hadn't known that).
Her mother had always carried on the know-it-
all—the real—conversations because she was the
one who knew about Camara Laye and Victor
Turner and Jung and Isak Dinesen and all the
books she and Piers could get excited about. She,
Rachel, had never actually had to think up subjects herself, so this visit now was strange, and
somehow got even tenser after her father came
home. The mixups got more embarrassing when
the houseboy set Piers a place for supper so Piers
ended up eating with them whether he wanted to
or not. She and her father and Piers were left in
the huge cold mud-walled dining room with the
airy late afternoon light filling every roughish
corner and making the room seem cavernously
empty, the three of them spaced out along the too-
long table. Her father was oddly quiet, not even
starting any Kabaka's sister's mother's brother's
stories. The light seemed to be catching an un-
settled, half-smiling nervousness in Piers' face.
She had never seen that face on him before and
after none of the conversation caught on the
silence seemed to crawl with hot wire nerves. Her
face caught the fire. She sprang up—anything to
break the dead-quiet suffocation. She dashed
outside. She marched wild-eyed in high wet grass
and banged her head against a papaw tree and
clutched at any reason she could tell him why
she'd run. Because she had to go back in. And all
she knew to say was that she'd had to go water
the flowers.

It was when they—her mother and Piers—
were putting on her mother's play that he was
most around their house. Her mother had written
it and Piers was helping her direct. They re-
hearsed most afternoons down in the chapel, just
at the time the school car came bumping up the
mountain back from Kampala (all the European

children on the hill and some of the Africans made
the long trip to Kampala every day). The car
would be beginning to dip and she could look
down then across the rolling lawns onto the
chapel with the hills and hills of bluish haze be-
yond and she could squint her eyes to will to Piers
to be outside where he could squint his own eyes
up through the sunshine and see her. And one day
he was actually standing in the shade under the
covered walk. The spot seemed dark across the
terraces of light. He glanced up at the car over his
shoulder, absentmindedly. Then he recognized her
and he spun completely around, stiff, not waving,
his hands in his pockets and with a great broad
grin. He bowed—bent way down from the waist
like he was bowing to the queen—with his stream
of black hair flopping down over his face. The he
stood back up and gave his hair the little jerk. His
hands were still in his pockets and he was still
grinning at her while she was unbuckling her skirt
already—exploding to get home and run back
down the hill.

She tore off her uniform. She pulled on her
grey-blue skirt that whirled in a full circle. She
brushed her hair and leaned across her dresser to
stare more closely at it in the mirror. Almost
curious she fingered the strand that hung down
her front because one time he'd played with it.

She headed quickly down the path and then
pretended calm when she approached the chapel.
He wasn't outside anymore. But she couldn't hear
them inside either. No one. She looked in the
door—her eyes still dazzled with the sun. The
church was shadows streaked with beams.

The silence put her at loose ends but she was
far too happy from his bow and too expectant to
go home. She wandered down the worn-brick
walk along the front of the college building. She
flamed a ridiculously brilliant smile when she
passed some student who didn't look any busier
than she did.

There was nothing against her walking along

the back of the hill. Even if that wasn't the place she normally went.

The wind was strong on his side of the hill. It billowed her skirt and streaked back her hair and pinned her blouse against her breast. Petals—purple—were blowing from a jacaranda tree and windy light was flaming everything to sparks.

She saw him. On the top of the hill coming toward her.

Her head spun quick with reasons why she'd come this way. But he didn't ask. He waited, grinning, beside the eucalyptus grove. He shouted "Come" because he needed her to help him carry "water-weathered" rocks that he was going to look for at the stream.

The wind was intoxicating. She could tell he felt it too because he grabbed her elbow like he'd never done before and sped her off so exuberantly that she was stumbling to keep up with him. He pulled her through the eucalyptus grove that suddenly was almost dark except for spears of yellow. The dimness caught a new and eerie silence with cicadas and leaves because the wind dropped when they went below the road. A sun daze opened at the bottom, and then they were at the sluggish stream and tramped around the edges looking for the right-shaped rocks and sat down near the pool of light beside the water. He was playing, joking, always, while she laughed but he was more than ever curious. He wanted to know about her home and family, everything about her mother and her father—what she remembered about them when she was very little. He had never asked her so many questions and she could feel his interest like a glowing circle all around.

She was sitting on a rock. Her feet were tucked under her blue-grey skirt and she was hugging her knees, shooing away gnats, looking down sometimes in blackish weed-choked water. Her hair was blowing underneath her chin and once he reached to pull it off her cheek.

He had settled on the reeds a foot or so away.

His knees, in his white pants, were pointed up and far apart and when he asked her something he jerked off his glasses and leaned back on his elbow, cocked his head and narrowed his eyes at her. Her answer wasn't bright. She was staring at the way his lips were so dark pink in the check-ered light and shade and the way they looked so soft and the way they seemed to be waiting—she could feel they were waiting, going to waste wait-ing—and with a sudden suicidal flash she leaned across and kissed them. Lightning quick. Playful. But having to put her face down on her knees.

He waited a moment. And when she didn't stir he stroked her hair. And then ultra slow he pushed himself up standing and he put his hands down in her armpits and he pulled her up and lifted up her chin with his hand and folded her against his chest and gently kissed her forehead and her nose and cheeks and eyes. And then he softly started eating in her lips. And she was terrified.

She shoved him back and ran. She crashed demented through the eucalyptus trees. She ripped her skirt and scraped her legs and leaped the fields and gulfs and hid.

For one whole day she avoided any spot where he could be. She let out squeaks that wanted to be screams. She couldn't grasp what she had done. She could never look at him again.

Until the second afternoon rehearsal time.

She had never walked right in on their rehears-als. She had hit before on sitting in a jacaranda tree that grew out of the high bank near the chapel. Sounds reached her there—the actors' fumbling, her mother calling "Cut" and jabbering on, Piers running flourishes on the piano and interjecting his quick laugh: the sounds had a spooky echo in the massive earth-brick chapel.

She loved the hidden seat. Nobody could see her unless they were directly under her but she could look out through the lacy jacaranda leaves and see the college buildings down the banks and

see the tiny isolated people in the blazing sun
where even blackness seemed absorbed in light.
And even if she couldn't see the rehearsal she
could hear the hollow echoings. She could day-
dream and wait.

There was, though, a little rough-brick vestry
room on the front part of the building opening off
from the church. She could look down into that
and sometimes she could see him.

One time that afternoon she did look down.
And she saw her mother and Piers kissing.

It was her muscles then and only her muscles
that knew enough to move.

But there wasn't any place for her.

She might have walked hours. She was farther
down the path than she had ever been. She
veered around anthills. She walked blind. A shape
loomed in her path but she held in her scream.
She ran before she knew what she had seen but
hulking things were everywhere: She couldn't tell
the anthills from the people or the clattering
hornbills from the darting obscure animals. She
stumbled back to walking where the path opened
again.

She could not go home. She picked her way in
aimless blurs.

She heard Luganda voices from a settlement
she knew. She was safe. She found a spot to
huddle in the bush in hearing distance.

She thought she heard a woman's shriek but
wasn't sure. She strained to listen. Even insects
sounded like a human wail. Sobbing noises came
and went and then began to sound like pulsing of
the dark that she had never heard before.

Her father would be searching for her, crazy in
his fear. She had to go back.

She trailed through elephant grass. She kept
missing her path. She forced herself to go inside
her lighted house, her foreign house. Her father
looked up from his book as if she were a ghost.
He'd thought she was in Kampala with her mother.

She dressed the next morning and she went to
school. She did the same the next day. She ate
and slept and moved and held books and no one
noticed that she wasn't the same person.
She never looked at her mother.

One day she walked to the dduka where the
dirt roads crossed. (The saucer-faced trader there
sold sugar and salt and flour when he had any.)
She knew Piers was behind her but she didn't turn
around. He didn't call out. They moved like
mechanisms.
She heard him speeding up. He was beside her
asking her to keep on walking past the stall.
Since the walking stayed awkward he decided
they should find a place to sit.
He pointed to a mound beside a guava tree.
It was a patch of nettles. They walked on.
"That banana grove?"
The mud was wet.
"Hey—over there." His spirits had a quick
rebound. He trotted ahead.
Ants covered the rocks that he'd picked out.
He grinned tentatively. There was elephant
grass or slushy growth. Or squatting in the ditch.
Or the peopled courtyard of a hut. A little boy in
a brown rag, naked under his navel, stared and
waved a reed at them.
He caught her hand and pulled her past a
curve and off to some rubbly murram where they
could sit. She knew she had to yank her hand
back to herself but she was flushed passive with
the feel of him and he had dropped it before she
got her force.
He fumbled then, saying he had meant to see
her, to apologize: "That afternoon . . . you mustn't
think . . . you mustn't think that I was only playing. You mustn't think it didn't mean anything to
me. But you are only fourteen years old and I
can't let myself feel anything for you no matter
what . . ."
He was looking at her with his trade-marked

look of intense sincerity.

She stared at that look. She saw he had no idea she could see straight through it. See he was lying. See he didn't know she knew about him and her mother. See he wanted to get out of this without a telltale mark on his beautiful skin. See he pitied her and that was like despising her.

She could make him stop playing. She could rip down to the truth. She looked away so she could dare to do it. She opened her mouth but before a word came out she was studying his face again.

She saw: When she threw his own self in his face all the thin glass world she knew would break. And she didn't want not seeing him. Whatever he was. In that moment she felt him like a weight in all her limbs. As if she weren't light—weren't a girl—anymore. As if she were a woman, leadened, a woman who couldn't any longer dart away from emptiness to water flowers, a woman who had to walk now with this dragging load of flesh. She closed her mouth. She studied the weed she was pulling from the rubble.

He was waiting. When nothing came he leaned down close to the side of her face and pulled back the strand of her hair so that his finger glanced her cheek and he said almost in a whisper, "You were going to say something."

She looked him full in the eye and shook her head.

Briar Patch

"Don't take yourself so seriously." Annie's words.

He stops the car with a jerk, spins around, says somewhat loudly, "You're talking to me just like your . . ." He's about to shout "just like your mother talked to you." But he catches himself, thank God, her mother being dead a mere three months. Still, he can feel Annie pulling away from him. He's begun to get scared of this new way of hers, this closing herself down, this shutting him out in a desert.

It isn't that he'd hated Annie's mother. The woman simply possessed some gentle, sugary manner of doing away with a person. Her mother was in the habit of suggesting, behind the victim's back, of course, that he took himself too seriously. Coming from her the line was laughable—from a woman who never had a whisper of a social concern, whose idea of the intellect was a non-stop game of bridge. That was the woman who handed out advice on how to be—meaning she had two absolutes, Annie kept informing him. Number one: Now you hold yourself up, darling. You got to remember to walk like a lady, darling. And number two: Don't take yourself so seriously.

The Southerner's creed in a nutshell—and look where it landed them. Blessedly, Annie escaped that pride-soaked decadence. Or so it used to seem. If her mother hadn't died and triggered this xenophobia.

Just now Annie is resolved he make the acquaintance of one of her multitudinous great aunts. That's the house they've pulled up to, the house of her Aunt Coles ("Colie" they say here— they seem to keep these women tied to senseless children's names). The house says every word that needs be said. It's a ruin, in a sea of overgrown bush. It's hidden under half-dead vines in a neighborhood turned neon drive-in hang-outs. Possibly once it was impressive—you can make out high arched windows and bits of classic columns on the stoop—not, mercifully, the puffed-up Southern-style column. But the paint has gone distinctly grey and peeling, the inch or two you see. It wouldn't take much to pull that tangle down, redeem this place. It apparently hasn't occurred to the occupant.

The spectacle is confirming his worse fears about this part of the world, and about what frightens him in Annie's new tendencies—Annie is his fiancé. When they first met Annie was as blazing angry at her South as he was but now she's come up with a whole new angle on herself—this family she still clings to—and who INVITES this rot, when all it would take would be a couple of hours of elbow grease to give this house a chance. This aunt of hers needs help, like ninetenths of the people he's stumbled on down here need help, big help, while here is Annie saying "Can't you see how I loved this place?" Her benighted nostalgia—deludedly teased out of pure and simple decay. But of course with the way he slipped up concerning her mother he can't let out a word of his authentic reaction.

It's his first time so far South. Chicago's his place. But in the case of Annie and him the twain had met quite amicably—they got together at Virginia colleges, neutral ground (compared, that is, to South Carolina). They both signed on with the winds of change, came close to getting in on a

sit-in, and now are off to India—first wave of
Peace Corps volunteers. They've come down here
to tie the knot before they get away for good. No
it makes no sense to have come all the way down
here, what with her mother dead already and her
father living up north. But the bee got in Annie's
bonnet, riding her new perversity.

A fat old dog barks casually, Annie calling him
Bowsie and patting him calm, Annie looking back
at him suspiciously like she's studying his reactions. Thank god she hasn't made a scene at his
faux pas. Now she takes his hand, leads him
around the side of the house to the hill of brown-
bush tangle. She says, "Aunt Colie has the same
birthday as me—she gave me birthday parties
here."

He says, "Parties in a bramble patch?"

She frowns him down, says, "Look. Just use
your eyes. Look at these paths—they weave under
and between and around every one of these
bushes. They make caves—see?—burrows, hide-
outs. It used to feel like you got lost forever. Like
nobody ever would find you. It was like you could
be Br'er Rabbit yourself."

Aunt Colie has discovered them, or Bowsie has
informed Aunt Colie of their presence. Annie runs
while he looks on. The woman is tall and thin and
bony with grey hair knotted in the back. The regal
woman decidedly walks like a lady—but whoever
thought of a lady in a baggy wooly sweater and
sporting saddle oxfords. It's not his idea of a great
Aunt Colie. She approaches him with her hand
out, grinning, welcoming ("Oh my dearest dearest
Ben") in the effusive way they have down here—
when she has never set eyes on him. He can
sense her scrutiny.

He follows the women and the dog inside.
Annie didn't warn him about the inside of this
place. The smell is musty—old leather at best,
mildew and unwashed dog at worst. The hall is
crammed with black and massive furniture.

Benches stacked with heaps of dusty objects, decaying piles of National Geographics. The rooms that open off this hall are shadowy—from the window vines blocking the light no doubt. The living room is glass-front ceiling-high cases of books, curly-legged marble-topped tables, worn-through covers on claw-legged chairs, one upright piano obscured under photographs and heaps of folded-back magazines. And what must be the woman's nest—a chair with a reading arm and lamp, scattered with papers and glasses and pens. Nondescript prints on the wall and a couple of blackened portraits.

The women settle on the curly-que sofa, the two of them holding hands and grinning, Annie repeating her demented happiness that nothing at all has changed.

Won't they have some coffee? The aunt heads for the kitchen and Annie pulls him up, leads him back through the spooky hall to what she calls the studio. Annie'd told him about it: Aunt Colie paints portraits—to keep food on the table. Portrait painting is acceptable painting in Columbia, but Aunt Colie studied real art, and in New York City. The family was suspicious of art, and of New York City. They made her come back South—her invalid brother had to be nursed, and Colie had "no obligations, being an old maid." She came back South. Somewhere along the line she stopped fighting that fact, hid her real art in the closet, and adapted. For forty years her companion, her patient, was her incapacitated brother, until he gave out on her a mere two years ago. Annie'd always wondered at the idea of this woman—couldn't imagine how Aunt Colie could have simply folded up her life—how anyone dared to ask her aunt to quietly abandon existence. It was part of what, once, made Annie hate her South. Understandably.

A portrait sits on an easel in a few left-over feet between the further piles of junk. It isn't bad,

as the portrait genre goes—loose brush strokes of
a black-eyed girl. But the painting room is
scarcely lighter than the other rooms in the house.
It has no curtains, which ought to mean good light
but the panes are grimy and of course the vines
are crawling all over the windows—rotting
screens, rotting everything (was it this woman's
despair, allowing this crumbling? She didn't
appear despairing, but how could she not see this
muck?) All it would take for decent light would be
one soul with some good old Yankee energy,
enough spunk left to yank down vines and throw a
little water on windows.

Back to the living room with coffee, Aunt Colie
in high gear, Aunt Colie delivering a comic run-
down on how he'd better prepare himself before
he faces this phalanx of Columbia judges, what
with Annie's mother's fifty-two first cousins. Aunt
Colie's wisdom: "Don't you mention that Chicago
word. You just say real sweet, 'Why I hail from
Virginia.' And," says she, "you invent yourself
some hunting stories—all about the deer you shot
that had those sixteen points." Annie is laughing,
and then in one of those silent interludes that falls
down over people, Annie jumps in with her over-
whelming question. Annie says to her aunt: "Are
you ever glad you came back
South?"

Aunt Colie says, "Sweet Annie, whoever taught
you to come up with such questions?" Then the
woman takes a minute or so, makes faces, says,
"Let me see if I remember so many hundreds of
years back. Oh yes yes I couldn't forget—because
I cried for ten —twenty—thirty years or so when I
had to give up everything I'd aimed for and scuttle
back down here—who ever heard of a painter in
South Carolina? Does that answer your question?
No, of course it doesn't. You're right, you're right.
I'll tell you just as honestly—I'll tell you exactly
why I HAD to come back South. I could TALK
when I got back down to this place. You know, up

there I'd make some remark, some pleasant trifle, like once when I found out a woman was sick and still working herself in the grave—and I said, 'I scream and yell for any help I can get when I feel the tiniest headache and here you're so quiet I had no idea you were dying' and the woman says back to me, 'Well, I'm not constituted to act that way. I believe it's very bad to complain.'"

Annie starts glancing at him and nodding her head knowingly.

"So there I been," this aunt now dropping into what sounds to him like a Negro's rhythm of talking, "there I been just putting myself down. It's in our blood, just putting ourselves down— truth to literal meaning being far as Santa Claus from any talk worth the time o'day—me building this woman up like good talk means to do—and that starchy woman takes me at my word—lectures me on how I got to learn not to complain. And that madcap kind of scene played every time I opened my mouth. I'd say all my clothes were foul—just to make some sociable nod, and up in that country they be handing me brochures 'bout washing soaps to purchase."

Annie laughs and means to catch his eye. He can see her reaching back step by step to count up all their own little misadventures—between the two of them. He can feel that counting progressing in every word this great aunt speaks. And the woman's going on and on and on: "I might have been talking Swahili and they translating into Australian aborigine for all we could say to each other. I couldn't figure where I was some days. But then—when I get back home, here I'm laughing and clapping and comfortable—I don't have to get a lecture on it being bad to starve when I said I ain't eaten in weeks—oh I don't know examples, it's a feeling. But after a year or so I got it figured out—that life comes down to manner. Now I understand you young people still laboring under the notion that manner is a superficial word. But

it ain't so. Manner is everything. I learned. I tell
you I learned."

He takes to staring at the water-stained ceiling
and the bug-heaped chandelier. Annie might have
set this woman up—with both of them glancing at
him, with this woman lecturing him, a lecture
being precisely what she herself was not about to
bear.

He can't be expected to sit here under assault.

"You got to have some way of being easy with
people," the devious woman goes on. "Which
means you got to sometimes cotton on the thing a
person's meaning to say. Everybody needs themselves a little easy laughing in this life, and that
easy laughing comes back when I get back down
here. We talk the same tongue down here—
bearing in mind you keep off genuine subjects—
like art—like things our Annie asks! Keep away
from Annie kind of questions and it's fun. Life
don't hide in big ideas. And it ain't in big ambi-
tions. Why, you say, but where it hiding then? I
say it hiding in play with words. I say it hiding in
charm, hiding in looking at things slant. Tha's
where—it's hiding in the manner. Oh yes—it took
me a good bit of time catching onto these things.
But I got there. We get by—we get by in this life—
long if we grabbing these moments. We got to
enjoy these little bitty moments." And she pats
hard on Annie's knee while she glances signifi-
cantly over at him. While Annie's been nodding at
him this whole mad tirade long.

The aunt can't stop herself. She's saying,
"I know you two didn't guess you were in for a
hurricane. But you heard it now—We got to laugh
at ourselves." The woman exaggerates her Negro
intonation. "And somebody got to grasp we laughing at ourselves. How else we gonna have our
fun?" She keeps on patting Annie's knee and
giving him these glances.

Already he is half up out of his chair. He's had
quite enough. Already he's long oversat himself,

what with Annie's face heavy with meaning, Annie measuring the way he attends to her Aunt Colie. He says, "You have to excuse me—I need some cigarettes. I'll be back."

He ignores Annie's heavy frown—she knows too well he hasn't been smoking in weeks.

The aunt hops up, says, "Oh my dear Ben, please don't you let us drive you away. You do know, dear Ben, you know you must not believe one word I ever say. You heard me—I cried thirty years when I had to come back South. Believe me I know—it's your part of the world that gets things done, lets an artist exist, lets you sit with your Negro friend in the living room instead of hiving off to the kitchen. The way I'm talking—you have to know I've spent a lot of time digging up reasons for the fact I had to come back home. Don't you believe a word I say—you hear me?"

He nods, says he won't, says he's coming back and leaves.

His insides are twisted into a spring. He drives off rapidly, turns onto Devine Street, out of sight, pulls up and drops his head on the steering wheel. He has to get Annie out of here. This place is turning her against him before they get together. He can't last through the next few days and the wedding. Except—at least after that he'll have her neatly away. He'll have her where it's clean— where there's light, where things are clear and black and white with no bugs heaped in the lamps—where there aren't devious twisted deadening vines blocking out the sun. Where you can hope to breathe. Where people say what it is they mean. Where things aren't expected to come out slanted, crooked, sideways. Annie gets along out there—in the real, decent, straightforward world— he's seen her—it'll work. As long as he keeps her out of this quicksand of a country.

Abruptly he sits up—replays the scene where he's just run away, where he's acted like a fool! He's made a colossal faux pas! His running away will hardly help him now. Annie'll think him a barbarian—if she doesn't already.

He stops before he reaches the house. He stares at that shrouded once-beautiful building and it hits him—what he must do. What he has to do to please Annie. He has to help this woman Annie loves! The woman's not strong enough to do what has to be done and here—right here in front of his eyes—is the one colossal need that he can fill. Prove to Annie he's a helpful soul. Prove to Annie she needs him around.

He gets out quietly, quickly, with a step gone light. He avoids the spots where the women might see through the window. He sneaks around the side of the house, around to what he knows is the studio—he will start at the painting room where they will not hear him, not till he has the whole house done—and then they can come see. He grabs at the ivy on the wall and he starts yanking rapidly, yanking the creepers off the screens, yanking the trails down off the boards. Quickly, as quietly as he can but quickly quickly, back along the side and now along the front of the house— letting in the light. Skip it that his hands are going raw—the aunt will have some clean fresh light on things.

The women come out the door and stop. Staring. He pauses a minute, hugging vines, and smiles.

Annie does not return the smile. Annie says, "What in the world are you doing?"

He says, "I'm letting in the light. I'm helping your aunt—saving this place—or else the boards will rot. It has to be done. I thought I could be useful."

Annie says "Ben . . ." and starts out across the weeds towards him, walking not at all like a lady. Scowling, her arms wrapped around her chest. Of course she won't be reasonable.

Abruptly he sits down. Hopeless. On the ground right where he is. His hands still clutching the ivy.

The great Aunt Colie comes loping down her steps and across her tangle of yard. She's calling out, "Annie, you wait now, Annie."

And then the aunt sits down on the ground beside where he is sitting. The aunt looks up at the windows he's pulled clear, says, "I know you're getting the notion I don't appreciate this, Ben. But you're wrong. I do. I am deeply grateful to you. For years and years I been thinking I got to do something about these vines creeping up over my windows. And these clean boards—now we gonna be able to see this house. It's a good house, first house here in Shandon, Annie's great-grandmother's house. I mean this house to last. Of course I can't let you come down here and labor—but you can't know how I appreciate this prod at our own laziness. I can't tell you what a help this is. I thank you sweetly and I thank you muchly muchly. I'm happy it's you—going to be my treasured great nephew." And the great aunt smiles at him.

He looks at this old woman with a mocking curiosity. She's lying every syllable she speaks. He's certain of that, and he is fascinated. This woman's graciousness is overflowing its bounds. He likes this woman immensely. If she can go so far as make him halfway believe her words, like she is managing just now, if she can make him like her half as much as she is managing, the woman is a blooming genius.

Annie is standing over them. He dares look up at her. She is biting her lip with a decidedly tense expression. He closes his eyes at her, acknowledging he understands. No he doesn't get this too-weird style of being, but he grasps the essential thing—grasps Aunt Colie has a right to whatever style she chooses without her life being taken over one more time by a meddler. Acknowledging he is aware of his offense—Annie needn't open her mouth to tell him his offense. He even grasps—almost—the reaction he's brought out in this bizarre Aunt Colie. And then he opens his eyes, on Annie, and begins to laugh. It's a very light laugh, but it's a genuine one. He sees her strained lip-biting turn into laughing around lip-biting, and the light comes back in her eyes. It feels like the easiest laugh that they have had together. It comes bearing a whole new view with it. It feels, suspiciously, like a baptism into this briar patch of her country, like almost beginning to enjoy these shadow-plays and games and lies and labyrinthine deprecations. And outlandish grace.

On Scott Gould

by Bret Lott

I LOVE SCOTT GOULD'S WRITING, AND THE STORIES COLLECTED HERE CONSTITUTE A BEAUTI- FUL AND MOVING AND HAUNTING TRIPTYCH OF MR. Gould's voice and vision, his unmistakable angle of perception, one that illuminates the human condition and graces our lives with its presence.

His voice is unmistakable in this: He presents us these worlds—a man's lifelong struggle with envy and love for his best friend and greatest nemesis, a young woman's flight from a life that seems perilously close to suffocating her, and the confused and confusing state of adolescence and race relations here in the South—all effortlessly, all in a diction that speaks truly and wholly out of the fabric of genuine charac-

ters. You will find nowhere in these three stories even the vaguest hint of the author's hand in the evocation of place, the rendering of dialogue, the movement of people through the paces of their lives.

Instead, what you'll find are real, genuine, living and breath- ing people faced with their lives and how they then might live. This is grace, my friends: the way Mr. Gould can give us sto- ries that seem not to have been written, but simply *are*, as though "Bases," "Nothing Fazes the Autopilot," and "Sort of a Prophet" were heirlooms kept under lock and key for a while,

only to be discovered by Mr. Gould and given to us readers in an almost benevolent gesture of faith that we will see in them the same sort of care and love and fear he first found in the writing of them.

And it is in this manner, finally, that the stories are given their greatest power: Because the storytelling capabilities of Mr. Gould are so everywhere eminent, and because his hand is nowhere evident, we have no choice but to be pierced by the truth of our humanity, of our own folly and triumph and stasis. Because the stories are so true in their telling, the truth at their hearts is made even more evident.

I know now I'm starting to sound like I'm talking in circles, and I may well be. But because Tolstoy once wrote that all great works of art have a single point upon which all things converge, or from which all things emanate, that that point must not be de-scribable in words, I know that this conundrum I am facing here—trying to put into words Scott Gould's work as a means of introduction—is all the more evidence of the art we have here with us.

All that remains, of course, is for you to receive the truths of these stories firsthand. To read them, and find in them the beating heart we all of us have, whether we have listened to it or not. Trust in this, however: Scott Gould has been listening, keeping track, through these tales of how we now live, in the most careful and beautiful way.

—Bret Lott is writer-in-residence at the College of Charleston in South Carolina. He is the author of four novels and a short story collection. His most recent work is Fathers, Sons, and Brothers, a memoir about the men in his family.

Bases

Back then, there were always two, maybe three black boys on the other side of the tracks that ran alongside the first-base line. The tracks were raised above the field on a steep hill, so they would lie flat against the slope, waiting for the train to come through on its way from the paper mill. When it did, they would lob rocks at us from behind the steady rush of cars, and we'd run to our dugouts until the caboose passed by and the man in the window waved. By then, of course, the black boys would be nowhere in sight. The umpire would holler and start things up, and as soon as we picked the rocks out of the field, we would be baseball players again. In the stands, the people—mostly mothers and fathers—just sat and looked over their shoulders at the tracks, in the direction of Nickeltown, where all the black people lived. It was just something that happened.

One afternoon, early in the game, we were already way ahead. I could smell the creosote railroad ties cooling down after a day in the sun. Someone had turned the lights on. I could hear the bulbs buzzing above the field. The train blew a warning at the far end of town, so some of the parents stood up and tried to wave us off the field, before any of us even saw the locomotive.

Be smart, they were saying to us. Get off that field before you have to make a run for it. We grinned and waved back and acted like big leaguers. We spit pink bubblegum juice in the dust and chattered at the kid standing at home plate.

The locomotive churned behind first base. We knew we could probably get in a couple more pitches before the rocks started. The noise from the train spun everything into a kind of dream. Mouths moved, but the only sound was the clank and groan of the cars on the rails. The umpire jerked up his arm and screamed, but you couldn't hear the call. Parents tried to yell at their boys. Then, it started.

Our third baseman ran by.

"Niggers."

He mouthed the word carefully against the noise from the tracks.

The rocks fell in lazy, heavy arcs, so slow you could dodge them easily as you ran to the dugout. I headed in from shortstop, kept my eyes up, and saw the caboose pass by. Short train. Less time for them to throw. That was good for the slower guys, the dumber ones who couldn't run and watch the sky at the same time.

But above us on the rails, in the fumes the train left behind, was one of the black boys in full sight. He was big, and stood facing us, cocked up a little on one hip, his arms at his sides. He peered down into the field for a second, then began his windup from his huge pitcher's mound.

High leg kick.

Push off.

I saw the exact second the rock left his hand, and I watched his pitch spin through the air. It had no arc. Just a steady, straight line from the tracks to the field. I could almost hear the rock when it hissed over the dugout and caught Cal, our first baseman, in the face. Cal flopped across the foul line in the clay dust. The boy on the tracks flipped us the bird and jumped out of sight.

Cal's mother was on her hands and knees in the base path, looking at the ground, but screaming at us. "What are you gonna do!" she yelled. "Somebody?"

Most of us were a few feet away, keeping her at a

safe distance as though she had a disease. But right beside her, our coach balanced Cal like a drunk, holding him up by his collar. Cal didn't know where he was, but he could mumble and sort of stand up.

"There ain't a thing to do, Louise," one of the fathers said from the crowd. "No way we can find out who done it, and ain't a one of us 'bout to go poking around Nickeltown looking for one nigger that hit a white boy with a rock."

It turned out that Cal wasn't as bad off as he looked. One of the mothers in the stands, who was a nurse, said that it would probably only take a dozen or so stitches and wouldn't leave much of a scar.

Cal's momma kept screaming, and our coach couldn't decide if he should bring Cal and leave Louise in the base path, or if he should try to carry them both. From where I stood, they looked like a family that couldn't make up its mind. One of the mothers walked over and grabbed Louise under her arms. "Now, now. It's over. Let's take Cal to the doctor and get him sewed up, OK?"

Louise screamed. "I want to know who did it! Don't you want to know?" She stuck her head up and watched the crowd.

Some folks nodded their heads and some couldn't care less. Some just wanted to go home. It was no big deal to me. I'd seen that guy before. Twice. I knew all I wanted to know about him.

The first time I saw him was in broad daylight at the baseball field. I always came early to the field, got the key to the equipment shed from A.J., and marked off the foul lines. It was really A.J.'s job to line off the field and cut the grass and hand out ping pong paddles at the Youth Center, but he spent every afternoon on his stool in the back door of the building, drinking bottles of warm beer, looking down the hill at the baseball games. He conned some of us into doing his work for him. "It's development," he told us. "I'm letting you develop valuable skills."

By that summer, I was so developed I could lay

down a straight chalk line without having to stretch a string to follow. I'd get the key from him, open the shed near the snackbar, take out a bag of lime and the rusty push machine. Then, I'd mark off the difference between fair and foul. It was an easy thing to do if you focused your eyes on something way up ahead. If you were at home plate, you needed to look out to the corner of the outfield. Then you walked slow. But if you kept your eyes on your feet and watched the lime trickle out of the machine, you would wander all over the baseline.

The afternoon I saw the black boy, I was almost to the outfield grass, dropping the trail of lime behind me, when I smelled something. It was different. It wasn't the lime dust or the railroad ties or the mowed wild onions. It was cigarette smoke, which isn't all that strange. But it's not something you expect on a little league baseball field. I turned around, and between me and home plate, the big black boy was smiling at me, dragging one of his bare feet in the dirt, erasing my line. The butt of a cigarette dangled from his huge grin. He wore a pair of blue jean shorts split way up his legs and no shirt. It looked like he had rubbed some of the new lime on his chest. I could see two white hand prints smeared across his belly.

I took off after him, but before I could make up any distance, he had already jumped the fence near the dugout and started up the hill to the tracks. When he reached the top, he didn't look back. Just leaped out of sight like a man going off a cliff. Except he was laughing.

I redid the part of the line he erased, and that evening during the game I could still smell his cigarette smoke hanging like a cloud in the thick air over the field. There were no trains that night, so no rocks, but I could feel all of those black boys, feel them watching us play our game, somehow blowing their smoke over the rails and into our field inning after inning.

When the game was over, I remembered I still had A.J.'s key tucked in my sock. I took it back and found him in the back door of the Center, staring down at the baseball field. "Don't forget to turn off the lights," I told him. There were times when he fell asleep drunk in the Center and the lights buzzed and burned all night, driving the moths crazy until daylight.

"I won't," he said. Then, "What would you have done?"

"What?"

"What would you'd done if you'da caught that big nigger today?"

The cigarette smoke filled my nose again, and I glanced over my shoulder just to make sure we were alone. All I saw was the glow from the field. "I guess I didn't think about it," I said.

A.J. took a pull from his bottle of beer. "You need to. You catch him, what you gonna do with him?" He finished the bottle and slung it toward the lights.

Sometimes, I can see what's going to happen. Tomorrow or maybe the next day, someone would run over that bottle with a lawnmower, and the day after that someone else would cut his foot on the glass.

I saw him again, a few days after he erased the foul line. It was in the woods near my house. I spent a lot of time there, high up in the sycamores and oaks, smoking reeds, the kind that grew straight up through the dead leaves on the ground—about as big around as a pencil, and hollow, like a straw. Once they died and turned brown, you could break them into little cigarette-size pieces, light up the end, blow out the flame and puff it while it glowed. I always headed for the trees where nobody from the neighborhood would think to look, and if it was humid enough in the woods, you could shoot out a gray cloud of smoke that settled into the limbs of the hardwoods like a fog.

One afternoon, I left the house with a book of matches, and a hundred feet into the woods, I had gathered enough reeds for an hour of smoke. For some reason, I didn't climb a tree. Instead, I just went deep enough into the woods to feel safe and sat at the base of a huge oak. I lit up, closed my eyes while the smoke swirled over my teeth, and I heard somebody laugh. I jumped up before I opened my eyes, but when I did, he was there, maybe twenty yards in front of me. Big and sweating, he seemed comfortable with the heat in the woods. I was choking on the smoke, the thick reed smoke that I never usually swallowed, that was now deep inside my lungs. He laughed once more, then reached in his pocket. Out came an old brass lighter and a pack of Camels. He lit one up, blew the smoke out of his nose and walked through the trees toward the tracks.

I started having dreams where the two of us met again in the woods. He carried a baseball with him, an old one that was scuffed and yellow with age, and he showed me the autographs on the cover. Black ballplayers who had signed just their first names with a pencil in a grade-school style print. I told him I'd never heard of these players, and he laughed at me behind a fresh Camel. He had a glove, too. An old one not much bigger than his hand. It smelled like mildew and saddle soap. I followed him to an open spot in the woods and found a pitcher's mound made of Spanish moss and, sixty feet away, a wide pine stump for a catcher to sit on. There was a straight strip of chalk line that ran from the mound to the stump. He told me this was where he practiced.

But we're on my side of the tracks, I said.

He laughed again and said that those tracks wasn't nothing but a couple pieces of steel on a hill, and he and some of his friends took turns with a shovel and dug a big tunnel underneath the tracks so they could come over here and throw the baseball in the trees. I started to tell him about how I climbed the trees here and smoked reeds.

The black boy stopped me and said, I don't wanna hear no shit about you and your trees. You ain't nothing to me.

He kicked at the lime with his bare foot, then he climbed the moss mound and wound up, the same

slow windup I saw that evening on the tracks above
our baseball field. He pushed forward and let fly, and
the ball rocketed through the trees—through the
center of the thick trunks. The trees bent from the
force of the pitch, like saplings in a hurricane. And if
you walked behind him and looked over his shoulder,
you could see a straight line of holes, all the size of a
baseball, and the holes seemed to go for miles and
miles, until they disappeared into a single dot of
darkness.

      We were all playing kick the can after dark.
That's what we told our parents. The only reason
they ever let us leave the house after dark was that we
told them we would be playing at Kathleen Simpson's
house. Kathleen's daddy was the Methodist preacher,
and most of our parents thought that his connection
with God would protect us once the sun went down.
What they didn't know was that that Rev. Simpson
slept in front of the television, and we pretty much
had free run of the huge back yard. Kathleen's house
was a few blocks on the other side of the Youth Center, so it was a long ride on my bike, but the dogs that
usually chased me couldn't see me coming in the
dark, and there weren't any hills. Just a straight shot
along the tracks and into Kathleen's yard.
      Cal was there with his bandage on. It had been
maybe a week or so since the thing with the rock. He
hadn't been back to the baseball field, but it was so
close to the end of the season, his momma was making him sit out until next year, when everything would
be healed up and in the past. He was just supposed
to watch and not sweat on his stitches. What he
really did was wander through the yard in the middle
of our game, while everyone else tried to stay hidden
behind the hedges. He talked and gave away all of the
hiding spots. He was just mad that he couldn't run or
do anything. He was mad about the blood and the
thin scar he was going to have. He was mad that his
momma screamed and crawled around the infield on
her hands and knees in front of a crowd.

Somebody said we should have a seance since we couldn't play kick the can. Kathleen ran inside her house and took a piece of candle and some matches from the kitchen drawer. She dripped some wax in the grass, stood the candle up straight, and we sat in a circle around the flame. We'd have to hold hands eventually, so everyone jockeyed for positions. I ended up with Kathleen on one side of me and Cal on the other. Then, we tried to decide who we wanted to call back from the dead. We went through the usual list for this kind of thing: Kennedy, George Washington, Marilyn Monroe, crazy relatives, rich relatives. Kathleen pushed hard for Marilyn. She said she was mysterious and tragic.

"Hitler," Cal said, almost in a whisper.

"What?" I said.

"Hitler, Adolph Hitler. We need to talk to Hitler," he told us.

Kathleen said, "What you want with Adolph Hitler?"

Cal stood up. "Look at this shit," he said, pointing at his cheek. I didn't look up, but I knew what he meant. "I got this and I can't do nothing about it. If I could get Hitler here, I'd tell him everything."

"And then what?"

"Hitler wouldn't let no nigger get away with this. Everybody else might, but ain't no way Adolph Hitler'd let us get rocks chunked at us every time a train comes by," Cal said. I turned toward him. With just the little flicker of light from the candle, I could see how shiny his face was. He looked like he was going to sweat right through his stitches. "Hitler'd go over to Nickeltown and kick some butt," he said.

I wanted to laugh. No matter how mad people got, they still called it Nickeltown. Nobody ever said Niggertown even though everybody knew that's what it meant. Instead of laughing, I said, "I think it might be a little hard calling Hitler back."

From the shadows on the other side of the circle: "My daddy says he ain't really dead."

"I don't care." Cal was breathing hard now. He was walking around the circle, having some trouble talking. "I want them people over there taken care of." He stabbed his finger toward the tracks. "Line 'em up and take care of 'em."

By then, some of the other kids were beginning to like the idea of having Hitler back in the land of the living. Hitler was no Marilyn Monroe. He was no mystery. Everyone knew exactly who he was. We'd heard the stories of Hitler, how he bombed or shot or burned down the things he didn't particularly like. He would have no trouble destroying Nickeltown, turning it into a pile of ash and hot tin. Cal would probably show him the quickest way across the tracks. Once they got there, I knew they would be able to find the black boy, and I imagined what would happen when he came face to face with Hitler. I stared at the candle in the circle and wondered if he would laugh and blow smoke at Hitler's head.

I don't want to hear no shit about you, the black boy might tell him. You ain't nothing to me.

I said to Cal, "You know these things ain't for real. Hitler ain't coming back."

"I aim to get me this nigger," he whispered.

"Just 'cause you're too slow to get out of the way of a rock ain't no reason to send some ghost of Hitler across the tracks," I said under my breath.

Cal came around the circle at me. "Slow's got nothing to do with it. You afraid what might happen if I get Hitler back here? You a nigger lover or some-thing?"

Before I could say anything, Cal spit on me. I saw it coming from up above me, like a tiny, gray bullet in the candlelight. But I couldn't dodge it. It hit me softly below the eye.

"See?" he said, wiping his chin carefully so he wouldn't disturb his stitches. "Slow ain't got nothing to do with it." He ran toward the street, in the direc-tion of his house.

For a couple of minutes no one said a word. They all watched me wipe my face with my T-shirt. Kathleen finally said, "I'd just as soon not have Hitler in the back yard anyway. Besides, if he isn't really dead, we'd just be wasting our time. We know Marilyn

Monroe's dead as a doornail, so why don't we call her back?"

Kathleen tried her best to make Marilyn appear. She talked up to the sky. I was listening hard, trying to hear if Cal was really gone. A breeze blew out the candle and Kathleen dug her fingers into my palm. But Marilyn never showed. Rev. Simpson came to the screen door and yelled at us. Told us all to go home and say our prayers.

I pedaled for home, keeping an eye out for dogs that might run from behind hedges. And for Cal, too. I thought he might be worked up enough to try something, even though he'd already spit on me. A block from the Youth Center, I noticed the glow, a dirty layer of gold that spread out in the air above the trees. A.J. had left the lights on again.

I propped my bike at the front of the Center. It was dark inside the building, but I'd been there enough to know where all the ping pong tables were. I weaved toward the back door and there sat A.J., leaning back a little on his stool, several empty beer bottles scattered at his feet. He was gazing off in the direction of the field. He tipped a bottle to his mouth.

He didn't turn when I walked up and stood beside his stool. He just kept staring at the field and said, "He showed up. Outa nowhere. Showed up and started."

I looked down the slope. The black boy was there, under the lights. He was running the bases with his shirt off. He was barefooted. He was playing his own game. He would stand in the batter's box, check his stance, and swing at an imaginary pitch. Then he would head for first base, round the bag, and try to stretch it into a double. I saw him slide, hooking his shin perfectly on second base.

I could barely hear his feet padding on the infield. The sound coming so late after the sight made me think that this wasn't really happening. The black boy was all of the batters, the whole team. Sometimes he struck out. Once, he hit an imaginary home run and rounded the bases in a slow trot. He waved to the crowd. He waved to the tracks. I think he waved at us.

A.J. took another, longer sip and let the bottle drop to the floor. "What you think we should do?" he asked me. But I didn't answer, just kept my eyes on the field.

Sort of a Prophet

We are early in this town, but far enough into
morning that the thin dew on the camper window
dries in the sun. I see where someone, probably some
boy, wiped a love letter in the dampness the night
before. It says

I love louise so

So what, I think.
In the dark, Louise's lover boy wrote messages
above our feet while we slept. Sleeping in the bed of
a pick-up, even with a camper top over your head,
opens you up to the worst of the night, to the lonely
boys and wet air that settles on the windows. I shiver
when I imagine it.
"Rabbits running 'cross your grave, girl?" Skyles
asks me, watching my shimmy as he wheels the truck
into a parking space on the street. An older cousin.
He is my third cousin who selfishly loves his long,
thin beard that happens to be a different color than
any other hair on his body. Already, even this time of
the morning, he twists and fidgets behind the steering
wheel, trying to find a comfortable position for his
legs. He says his legs are in a sad condition, that he
can't keep the right amount of circulation in them.
Always on the road after breakfast, he drives for only
an hour or so before asking me to take over. Sometimes he crawls into the back and stretches out, so
his heart can have a straight shot at his feet.
I knew a girl in high school who suffered the same

way. She owned a heart that didn't have the right kind of power. It couldn't shove the blood as far as the tips of her fingers and toes. She always wore gloves and closed-toe shoes, even in the summers, but sometimes, especially when she'd had a few beers (which, of course, thinned out her blood), she whipped off her shoes and socks and gloves, then showed off her blue hands and feet like a carnival attraction.

She told me winters were the worst, that when it turned really cold, the blue snuck up to her wrists and ankles. I dreamed once that she woke and her entire body was the color of sky in September, and she heard her heart laughing between beats.

I wonder about the state of Skyles' heart when he complains of his legs. And that is the only matter of his heart that concerns me. My mother, naturally, guessed his was dark with sin when the two of us rode away in the truck. She spit out the words "black" and "sin" in the same sentence, figuring, I suppose, that I would come knocking on her door one evening, my arms wrapped around my sleeping bag and a baby born too near the family tree—an almond-eyed boy who would mumble to himself and rock on his heels every day of his life. I knew it was a waste of time to tell her that my cousin had nothing to do with sin or love, and I was instead driven away by the idea of connecting dots on the map, dots that before only swam in front of my eyes when I stared too long at cities on paper.

"It's the damp," I finally answer, shivering again. "It gets in and I can't shake it."

"The heater's been going for the last couple of miles. Why don't you beam that vent on your feet. You lose some of your warmth through the feet, you know."

He knows a good deal more than me, though to look at him, you might guess he's one of those men who stop trying to find out new things at a certain age or after a certain event, like the first time they hit someone flush in the face or the first time they really start sleeping with somebody. Some men decide there isn't any more need to learn. But Skyles gathers bits of information like some people collect old bottles. He holds onto things most folks throw out, sticks them up in his brain and pulls one out when he needs it. At breakfast, he reads all the household hint columns and doctor's advice so he can file away something new.

For a lot of people, he appears too smart or too mysterious to be dumb. With the long beard and the way he walks stooped over like a man with some heavy years on his back, he might be sort of a prophet. Once, when we were in New Mexico, a woman tangled up in a blanket at the campground asked him dozens of important questions, all of them beginning with "why." At the end of each question, her voice rose, then disappeared into the folds of the blanket. She laughed at us when we walked back to our campsite, embarrassed that Skyles said nothing, did nothing but stroke his beard.

We do attract stares when we go where people can see us. Skyles, because of his beard and his gait, and me because I'm too tall and flat-footed, and tend to forget I'm a woman until Skyles reminds me in the middle of the night or God reminds me in the middle of nowhere, miles from a drugstore. I wash when I remember to, and the rest of the time, I just tie back my hair and let people whisper what they want. I can't be bothered with men and women I'll never see again.

But Skyles always says, "The world ain't but a circle. People'll show up a second time. Somewhere." I say, I only have the time and energy to worry about the people I'll look at more than once.

Which is why I call Mother from the diner where we stop for breakfast. We always sit to breakfast because Skyles likes to prepare his legs for the long ride in the truck. With the two time zones between here and home, I know she will be getting ready for church, a bad time to call, since her mind will already be on sin. But on the other hand, Sunday morning is usually a sober period for her because she has to confront God and the congregation at the same time. I know she likes to put her best face on when meeting important people. I'm sure, though, that since I left, she's received more than her usual share of sympathy from the church regulars.

I call every week or so to give her the chance to spill her madness off over the phone, or maybe to hear her ask me if I'm in love with my third cousin. If she ever does ask, I will tell her that love's got nothing to do with how many times removed a man is from the family and nothing to do with smearing notes on truck windows. I give her these chances, but she never takes them. She treats me like a neighbor on the phone. She gossips about births and deaths, then finds a reason to end the conversation. We never do anything important over the phone. This time, the phone's busy over and over.

Outside, Skyles shakes a bottle of soda he has plugged with his thumb. After a couple of good jolts, he aims the bottle at the rear window of the camper.

"Carbonation's supposed to cut road film. Don't know how it'll do with window writing. I used to get whipped for this when I was a kid, drawing faces and such on the glass. Somebody ought to be whipped." He laughs a little.

"Leave it," I say quickly, trying to catch him before he lets go with his thumb, trying to avoid sounding panicked.

"I can't see out the back with all this."

"You never look out the back anyway. I'll be driving in a while, so leave it. It doesn't bother me at all."

He sticks the top of the bottle into his mouth, his thumb still stopping the hole, and lets the soda explode. His eyes water from the gas as he swallows hard to keep up with the foam.

"I don't know why you got to get so strange," he says. " 'Leave this,' you say, but you can't say why. It might've been good, you know—to see if soda cuts through window scribbling. One idea like that and next thing—bam! For all you know, spraying soda on the back window of a truck could've been the thing to make me a million. Damned if I'll let a woman and her strangeness get between me and a million dollars." He slams the door on his side and cranks the truck, then opens the door while the engine idles loudly.

"You drive. I'm upset now," he says and slides through the tailgate into the bed of the pick-up. From inside one of the rucksacks stashed against a wheel well, he pulls the round Boy Scout canteen he's saved for over thirty-five years. What he keeps inside the canteen changes day to day, but it all does the same thing. The canteen and the sound of the wheels spinning on either side of his head lull him to sleep. He'll rest until lunch, I know, and then he'll refill the canteen at some roadside store and spend the afternoon the way he spent the morning. It's good for the circulation problem, I suppose, but it bothers me that someone so committed to the road sleeps away so many miles.

Skyles is one of the few people I've met who can sleep when they're mad, and after twenty or so restless miles, I hear him snoring in the back. I count road deaths for a couple of hours—possum and curious dogs that wandered onto the pavement. The numbers amaze me. Skyles wakes up when I stop the truck for lunch and drinks the last of the canteen.

"Where are we?" he asks, clearing his throat.

"Half way," I tell him, which is nothing unusual since lunch is normally half way between breakfast and suppertime, when we stop for the night. Skyles walks up to the store and tries to buy a bottle from the man behind the counter. I imagine the man lecturing Skyles about it being Sunday, how in this state you can't sell liquor on Sunday, and how a drunk is easy prey for the Devil while everyone else is safe inside a church. When I walk by on my way to the pay phone, Skyles tells the man that without the proper liquids, he could very well die. He pulls a yellowed newspaper column from the collection he keeps in his shirt pocket. The article says that a touch of alcohol per day may actually prolong life. He quotes from the article.

The man ignores the fact that Skyles wants to add a couple of hours to his life. "How long it take you to grow that beard?" he asks.

The phone rings over and over at my mother's until I hang up and try again to make sure I didn't mess up dialing the first time. She must be outside, I imagine, wandering in the back by one of the rotted arbors that has been wrapped up and twisted out of shape by some vine Morey planted, then left on its own. Morey replanted the whole yard when he married my mother.

"I take it you know where you're headed today, huh?" Skyles asks when I return to the truck. He's sitting on the tailgate, pouring whiskey from a bottle into his Scout canteen like a careful chemistry student. He's not upset anymore, even pleased now that he convinced a stranger to break a law. "I mean, I'm giving you the deed to the road today."

He crawls back inside with his full canteen, and I seal up the truck and the camper top. The note about Louise has turned a chalky brown, brown enough to make me think her lover must be a tall man with an angry, heavy hand.

Before, in the morning, I saw him as thin and quiet, a boy who sneaks around with his feelings leaking through the tip of his finger like blood through a pinprick. Notes are the wrong way to find out what someone else thinks. I'm betting Louise never sees the back of our truck, never knows somebody loves her enough to write about it. I started to leave a note for Mother, one she would find hours after we put some miles between her anger and my fear of the road. But I didn't want anything to be underhanded. I left after lunch on a Friday when Morey was home from the bank. I wanted a witness and a pair of eyes for her to look into when she realized I was doing it, that it wasn't just a trip into town or a quick run down the road to dry the truck after a washing. A note would give her something to hold on to for a short time until it turned yellow or was lost. The way it ended up, she can see me go over and over when she shuts her eyes.

In the back, I hear Skyles banging through the boxes, looking for something to eat. I usually don't have lunch, but Skyles likes to eat lunch while he's mobile. He knocks on the window of the cab and holds up a wedge of orange stuck on the point of his pocket knife. He knows I hate oranges and have a fear of open knives, and the whole of it makes him grin as he slides the blade between his lips. I wish for a second that we were back in west Texas where the roads are so boring and straight they build sudden dips into the pavement, just to keep you awake. I pray for a bump as he picks his teeth with the knife point, his face pressed close to the cab window.

Once he eats, he rewards himself with a pull from the canteen and settles in for the rest of the afternoon. Around six, I find my way back to the little campground a few miles off the interstate. The fat man in the tiny store owns the campground, which is actually a bunch of dirt plots divided with railroad ties. A gravel two-rut runs down the middle of the camp sites. I already know the prices, so I have the money ready.

"Hold on," he says from behind the racks of beef jerky and cheese nabs. "Second night in a row ain't but a buck and a half, you know. I figure you gon' stay 'round, you mays well get a break somewhere." With the change, I buy a large packet of instant soup and a couple of pieces of soft bubblegum. Skyles needs something with a lot of quick sugar when he wakes up in the evening.

When I roll down the gravel, I try to remember how it was the day before, what's changed and who's left. Most camping places like this one are just for overnighters on their way somewhere, just a spot to sleep and nothing more. I find the same site we used the night before and open up the tailgate. Skyles moves, but only to shift to the other side of the pick-up bed. He probably won't eat the rest of the night and will only get up to weave into the trees to use the bathroom. I'm hoping Louise's man has more modern toilet habits because I spend the next couple of hours hanging around the entrances to the dull, cement block building that serves as the campground bathhouse. I'm back to see what a man alone and in love looks like. I'm back to look for Louise's lover.

The bathhouse is a sensible place to visit. That is, if he stayed the extra night, of course. I watch fathers holding their sons' hands as they carry towels into the shower and uncomfortable women with duffel bags of make-up and shampoo. I never see a man who looks like he has been hurt enough to write on a truck window.

When the people stop coming to the bathroom, I sneak in the men's side, just to see if Louise's name is popular in other places. After a minute, the door squeaks, so I latch myself into a stall and sit like normal.

The man bangs through the swinging door next to me and groans as he lowers himself. I feel safe because I'm wearing shorts and from the knees down, I could pass for a skinny man in the toilet. I see Skyles' hand-tooled belt buckle on the floor beneath the partition. I want to ask him why he used up all the effort to make it to the bathhouse, why he didn't hug the trunk of a tree like he usually does. He sits for a long time, long enough to make me think he brought the canteen with him.

I can't figure the noises I hear coming from his stall. It's not normal for where we are, not bathroom sounds or the whisk of clothes drawn up bare legs. It is a scratching, the kind of noise that comes from a kitchen at night when mice are out. I put my ear to the plywood partition and the scratching turns to raking—a harsh sound so close to my head. When I pull back and glance toward Skyles's feet, I see tiny shavings and flecks of wood the same dull green color as the rest of the bathroom.

Skyles continues to scratch until the belt buckle rises and he calls out over the top of the stall. "OK, neighbor, you win the award tonight."

He washes his hands in front of the mirror, and through the crack in the door, I watch him shuffle out of the room. It bothers me that he washed his hands.

I would have never guessed.

Inside his stall, the seat is still warm on the back of my thighs. To the left, in the plywood, I see the fresh carving that hasn't been dulled by the moist air in the bathhouse.

It says

louise hurt me good

Only when I finish my shower next door do I realize I don't have a towel, so I dry off with handfuls of tiny, rough paper napkins stacked on the sink.

The soup is thin, but enough to feed the both of us. Later, I lie staring, listening for someone to walk in the gravel outside the truck, until Skyles wakes up and rolls into my half of the sleeping bag. All I think of is his clean hands. They pin me down, then work their way under me, and I still listen for anything outside, in the trees or on the highway. Trucks, maybe, that can't afford to stop for the night, or the fat man, double-checking the lock on his little camp-ground store. On the breeze, I smell the creosote from the railroad ties.

The canteen is empty. "Where are we anyway?" he asks when he's through and back on his side of the truck.

For breakfast, we eat at the same diner as the morning before, and the waitress treats Skyles like a regular. He's confused and looks like he hasn't been let in on a decent joke, but he still thinks we covered some distance yesterday.

I call home from the phone in the back, beside the door to the kitchen. Through the port hole window, the cook on the morning shift samples something with two fingers—grits or cream of wheat maybe. The back door to the kitchen is open, and from where I stand next to the phone, I can see two dogs, brown and runny-eyed, lying belly down on cement still cool from the night, waiting for the cook's mistakes to sail over their heads and into the dust.

The kitchen looks too hot for this time of day, and I feel a thin rush of warm air escaping through the space between the swinging doors.

The phone is busy and I curse Morey. I know he's home. It's close to lunch time where they are, and Morey only knows two romantic tricks. Sneaking home at noon so he can push my mother back into the bed, and the other one—kicking the phone from the receiver as he rummages around in the sheets. My mother told me this when she was drunk. She said Morey does the same thing, the same way every time, and that's why he is a good man.

The steady clip of the busy signal reminds me of the sound of tires over the grooves in the concrete interstate, the way you can beat out time with the radio depending on your speed. I see myself on the highway alone, now. Thumb and chin both out. Even with the kitchen next to me, I can imagine the smell of the greasy-breathed trucker who will pick me up and ferry me from stop to stop. Or the college boy who needs an experience with someone who never has more than a first name. A girl may stop for me and wonder why I smell and why I travel alone. I may pull my hair under a hat and grab my crotch and pretend to be a man from a distance. I can see myself now, and I'm doing more than driving in circles.

Our food swings through the door and the waitress gives a nod toward the tray she balances, as if to suggest I'm running late and I'm on a schedule. The sight of the eggs and the biscuits with gravy turns my stomach, but makes me hungry at the same time. Skyles whistles, points to the food she sets on the table, and waves to me with the other hand.

It is easy now. I walk up and stand while I take a sip of water. He jabs his finger at the newspaper. "Will you look at that? One aspirin a day can keep you from having a heart attack. What do you know."

Still standing, I say. "One day I might have a baby girl. If I do, I'll name her Louise. I think Louise is a fine name, don't you?"

He waits for a minute, then smiles and turns his face into the newspaper, but I know he's not reading. I leave his smile dangling and walk through the kitchen door and by the cook, who sits in front of the open refrigerator in the flow of cold air. After I pass by, one of the dogs rises up and follows me, thinking I have something for him, until I chase him away with a rock.

Nothing Fazes the Autopilot

I used to piss on Dalton Weathers once every spring. Always during an early morning. I never really knew exactly what time it was, but one night in late April or early May, before I went to bed, I would drink a couple of large glasses of water, and when I woke up before dawn, I'd climb into my car—me and my pounding bladder—and drive to a private family cemetery on the bluff above the lake, and I let him have it in the dark.

On the way home, I felt better. Lighter somehow. Someone might have said that I went too far, that only a crazy man would leave his bed in the middle of the night to relieve himself on a flat grave marker, which by the way, is chipped on a corner from a lawnmower or the weather. Someone probably said that I should be happy with what I had.

I always visited the grave in the spring because when the weather warmed up, ten thousand weeds launched themselves in my back yard. This is not a wild exaggeration. You would think the weeds provided some sort of spectacle or tourist attraction, but it was not something to marvel over or take pictures of.

They all had names, these weeds. Parsley Piert, Dollarweed, Pennywort, Buckhorn, Shepherd's Purse, Chickweed and the ever popular Dandelion. Beautiful names, but I hated the fact that they were weeds. I tried to pick them by hand or slash them with a weedeater as soon as they appeared, but sometime during the night or in the morning just after sunrise, they got ahead of me. The Veronica and the Henbit. They grew in the rain. They thrived in drought. The Black Medic and Bittercress. The herbicides I used provided relief for only a couple of weeks. Cutting the yard helped for a few days or so until the next wave poked its head through what little grass I had. Once, I rented a tractor and plowed up the whole yard, but the weeds were back in a matter of days. It was during my yearly battle with the weeds that I was the maddest at Dalton, and this anger was what sent me to his grave.

Dalton used to be my neighbor, and he came home one night drunk, you see, and he knew I was vulnerable. He knew I could be dealt some sort of perennial blow because my back yard, my brand-new back yard, from the house down the small hill to the shoreline, was freshly tilled, muddy from rain, waiting for me to lay out the rolls of sod I had been planning to buy. I had become tired of seeing my property wash into the narrow cove of the lake that curved behind our houses, and I'd decided that the sod would keep things in place.

Dalton stumbled into his boathouse that night. (I say stumbled, but how do I know? I was sleeping, so all I can do is guess.) On the shelves that ran the length of the wall, Dalton kept mysterious jars full of seeds, jars I had seen many times. Thousands and thousands of seeds. I always thought it was a nursery under glass—color and beauty he was planning to free some day. Why he saved seeds, I never knew, because I never actually saw him plant anything. His yard was wild, left on its own season after season. I don't even know where he got his seeds. And I didn't know they were weeds.

That night, the night he got me, he must have filled a huge bucket with his seeds. Jar after jar, species after species of weeds. He mixed them with his hands when the bucket was almost full, and he let them trickle between his fingers like dry sand. Remember now, I'm guessing.

Our yards were separated (still are) by a thin creek that spills into the cove. Over the creek is a narrow bridge made of a telephone pole split lengthwise and laid open, flat side up. In the dark, he must have crossed the bridge by feel, trusting his feet alone to find their way to my muddy yard. And there in the dark, Dalton danced and slung seeds from one end of my property to the other, from the porch to the water's edge. In some places he was careful and spread the seed evenly. In others, he left little piles, like new anthills on the mud. Sure, I noticed the seeds, but what was I supposed to do? I thought they were flowers. I waited for an explosion of color. I was excited at what he had done to me. A neighborly gesture. I loved flowers.

Nothing, of course, happened for days. I had postponed my plans for the sod, because I was waiting for the perfect conditions to anchor my yard with grass. There was more rain. I even tilled some more, turning the soft dirt over on itself a couple of times. Dalton said I was trying to ruin his surprise. But we smiled at each other.

One morning I looked out of my back window, and Dalton was hunched over in the dirt, on all fours, pointing at the stalks and runners and renegade blossoms that had appeared overnight. He was laughing, shaking. By the time I walked downstairs and into the yard, he was up to four hundred and still counting.

Dalton's father killed himself farming. Even the rich soil in the river bottom, so rich they said you could plant your toenails and grow rows of new feet, couldn't keep him alive.

When times were perfect, things grew like crazy on their land, Dalton told me once, but big hail and late freezes and early frosts and fire and low prices had little respect for the smelly, black dirt. His father got tired of fighting the weather and the marketplace, and he began to drink when he should have been plowing or harvesting.

Dalton found his father stone dead from alcohol poisoning one afternoon, sitting upright on the back porch—his eyes dry and open, staring off into a field full of volunteer soy beans. Dalton was fifteen.

His mother shipped him to an uncle who lived nearby while she went off somewhere to look for work. Dalton says she must've found one hell of a job because she never came back, and she never sent for him. Two months after she left, the power company announced they were building a lake. They had plans to dam the river and flood the bottom land so they could light more lights.

Two and a half years after that, Dalton and I graduated from high school together. We were best friends, and we were alike in a number of ways, but the biggest difference between us was that Dalton owned almost ten miles of shoreline on the new lake. Even though he still lived with his elderly uncle, Dalton was rich. The richest senior in the history of Crescent High. He was a goddamned land baron. Once the lake had finally filled, it covered most of the farmland his father had let go to seed. What wasn't covered was expensive beachfront. And since his mom never showed up to claim her share, Dalton owned every foot of it.

We went to different colleges. Dalton sold a couple of his lake lots and was able to attend an expensive private school, even though his grades were a bit below mediocre. He shouldn't have been admitted with his record, but I suppose being able to pay four years of tuition—in full, in advance—makes you an attractive freshman. I went to the state school nearby. I even thought I would live at home to save a little money, but my parents decided to move back north once I graduated from Crescent. They both said the move was part of an unbelievable business opportunity for my father, but I knew better. They were running the first chance they got, fleeing to a home they'd left behind years ago. They had never liked the South. They wanted to go somewhere where the winters were long and beat the shit out of you and made you really appreciate the warm weather when it finally arrived.

"The weather in the South," they said many times, "will make you soft about life."

During the first couple of years of college, Dalton and I never really saw each other. He came home only once during that time, when his uncle died, but other than that, we were completely out of touch, even during the holidays and summers. I heard that when school let out every spring, he always went to the Midwest to work on the wheat or the corn, but I always thought it was funny he traveled so far for a job. I mean, you didn't really have to work at all if you owned shoreline.

Then Christmas of our junior year, he sent me a card. On the front was a tacky picture of Santa Claus zooming through the air, drafting behind his eight reindeer. Inside was a phrase, but I don't remember what it said. Something clever and seasonal, I think. Taped below the phrase was a color snapshot of an infant girl. Actually, it was part of a picture. Half of the photo had been trimmed away. The baby was bald and wrinkled and so brand-new looking that the picture could've been taken in the delivery room. On the back, there was a name and some info:

Raleigh Weathers.
b. 11/26/70
Blue eyes.
Have changed my major, as you can see.
Ha, ha. Dalton

Raleigh was the only memorable thing Dalton brought home when he dropped out of college. Just after her birth, he sold one of the swampy lots he owned for an ungodly amount of money and used the cash to build a house for his little motherless family. I didn't really have a home then. My parents had made it back to upstate New York, and I had no interest in visiting them. They were deliriously happy. They loved freezing and thawing, freezing and thawing. On

the other hand, I wasn't ready for cycles like those.
I was ready for the more unexpected things in the
world. The problem was, I was all dressed up with a
degree in history and had no place to go.

One night, right after my graduation, before I
packed up and left the school for the last time, Dalton
called.

"I have a plan," he said when I came to the phone.
He didn't tell me who was calling or how he got the
number, and it didn't matter that it had been years
since we'd had a real conversation. I knew right off
who was on the line, and he knew that I knew.

"You have a daughter, too," I said.

"She has colic. She only sleeps when she's ex-
hausted or when I give her a lot of cold medicine."

"You have—?" I asked.

"A plan. This is it: I want to give you a piece of
land. One right next to mine. You have to pay for
building a house or whatever it is you want to do on
the land, but you don't have to spend a cent for the
property. It's on the water and we'll be neighbors."

He said this in what seemed to be one breath, like
he knew exactly how long it would take to get the
words out.

He had practiced what he was going to say, I
thought. Probably practiced on his daughter.

So I took his deal. I knew what Dalton was doing.
He was trying to surprise me, trying to see how I
would react. It was something he did, for as long as
I knew him. It was his way of shaking up the world.
He wanted me to stutter or stammer or something,
and I wouldn't give him the satisfaction.

Anyway, I considered myself lucky, not just to have
been given a piece of prime shoreline, but also because Crescent High needed a history teacher. This
was during a time when banks still trusted school
teachers, and the local savings and loan gave me the
money to build a small house on the lake. For the
entire summer and into the fall, I slept in Dalton's
boathouse, on a cot below a shelf bowed with the
weight of seed jars. He said I should sleep out there,
that with Raleigh in the house, I'd never get a

minute's rest.

I began to learn how to teach history to young people who had very little past of their own. I watched my house go up. From my cot in the boat-house, I could see Dalton passing back and forth in the glow behind his upstairs window, walking his infant daughter in the hours before dawn.

We had these sessions on the dock, Dalton and I. We drank beer and threw small hunks of cheese in the water. Gray schools of tiny bream batted the cheese like a volleyball until one of the larger, more fearless fish sucked it into his mouth. Sometimes the fish would reject it and blow it out through his gills, and the volleyball would begin again.

"Dalton," I said, "who is Raleigh's mother?"

"Nobody you'd know," he said.

"Is she dead?" I asked.

"Terminal," he said.

"Does Raleigh know who her mother is?" I always pressed on.

"She has her doubts," he said.

Raleigh was one of the strangest girls I had ever come across. She never had anything to say, but always looked like she was on the verge of asking a question. She wouldn't talk to you at all, although it appeared she was dying to give you some piece of information. If you were around her enough, you would have seen this. You would have noticed her habit of leaning forward a little, even when she stood still. And she always inhaled deeply, like she was about to speak. Then as you waited, she usually sighed and decided that it wasn't worth the effort after all.

The only time I definitely remember her saying something was during class one afternoon. Advanced American History for juniors. For almost twenty years now, I have presided over roomfuls of teenagers while they butcher the great American moments since Plymouth Rock. But I am proud to say I only do history. I don't coach a team or chaperone beginning

drivers through town or head up the student govern-
ment. Just history.

History is safe. You can always change it to suit
your mood. And I can't burn out because I've been on
autopilot for the last five years. I'm the only teacher
I know who is burn-out proof. I'm a goddamn asbestos educator.

When Raleigh was in my class that year, I wasn't
worried about the staleness of my routine or my
performance, even though she lived across the telephone pole bridge and her father had ruined my yard
forever. I didn't know what she thought of me. I
suppose it didn't matter. She never spoke to me,
though I'd been over hundreds of times to see Dalton
while she lay sleeping in the sun on their dock.

She was the complete stranger who lived next
door, the one I watched grow up from a distance. I
did watch. I'll admit that. But there never was much
to see. I never saw a boy bring her home and kiss her
under the porch light. I never saw her sneak out to
the dock in the middle of the night and dive naked out
of sight. But I saw her name on my class roll that fall,
and I figured she'd have to talk during American
History. I mean, that's about all you can do with
history—talk about it.

But as hard as I try, I only remember one thing
she said during that whole year. We were discussing
Lizzie Borden one afternoon. (Every once in a while,
I throw in some bizarre event from the past, one with
a lot of blood and mystery to keep them interested
while I shift gears into something else, something
boring and important.) Lizzie was a favorite. Students liked the story. They liked the fact that Lizzie
used an ax and did away with her parents. Sometimes
they cheered Lizzie on when I recited the little song.

Lizzie Borden took an ax ,
And gave her mother forty whacks .
And when she saw what she had done,
She gave her father . . .

You know how it goes.

I was in the middle of the Borden story when Raleigh stood up in the aisle. She leaned forward next to her desk at the back of the classroom. It was close to Thanksgiving, nearly her birthday, I think.

"Raleigh?" I said.

The class spun together, like a dance troupe in their desks to watch her. Raleigh was going to speak. This had potential to be a rare event. She took a breath. She said nothing. This was normal. The usual fake. I looked down at my notes, so I could pick up my place. I really didn't think Raleigh would talk, so I waited for her to sit down again.

"She never said she was sorry." Raleigh spit out the words like they were sour.

Now, I was surprised, but I was on autopilot and had the autopilot look on my face—a dead stare. Nothing fazes the autopilot.

"Well, actually," I said, "what Lizzie Borden told everyone was that she didn't do it."

"She never said she was sorry about anything," Raleigh repeated and sat down. Then she said, "That's important, I think."

For ten minutes we all sat and stared at each other in the quiet. The autopilot and his children. There was no discussion because I could think of nothing to say. I remember a football player near the front had a bad cold and was whistling through his nose every time he took a breath. The bell rang and class was over.

One afternoon, the summer after Raleigh's junior year, Dalton suddenly had a seaplane. It was yellow and red and tied to his dock. It bobbed heavily in the cove like a giant fishing lure.

"Do you know how to fly?" I asked him.

"I know I like to fly," he said.

"What the hell kind of answer is that?" I said.

He walked down the gangplank toward his plane. "Well, I figure wanting to fly and wanting to learn how to fly are two all together different things. One takes a lot longer than the other. Anyway, I got this guy who's gonna show me how on the weekends. In-the-cloud-training."

Every Saturday, Dalton and his teacher, who never took off his dark glasses and was named Shaker, would paddle the seaplane to the rear of our cove. I took Dalton's aluminum boat out to the mouth of the cove, where it emptied into the big water, and I gave them an all-clear signal when there were no boats approaching their takeoff path. Shaker revved the engine, blew up some spray into the trees, and they were off in a loud show of wind and waves.

Where they went, I never knew, and Dalton never told me. They would just return a couple of hours later, land in the lake and taxi up to Dalton's dock. From my house, I'd see Dalton give Shaker some money, pat him on the shoulder, and the plane was pretty much forgotten about until the next Saturday, when they would ask me again to be a lookout for their takeoff.

One Saturday, only Dalton approached me. Shaker wasn't anywhere around.

"This is my solo," Dalton said, reaching into the cockpit for his paddle.

"Do you know enough about this?" I asked him. I suppose if I had been a true friend, I would have tried to talk him out of it. Or maybe if I was really his friend, I wouldn't have even brought up my doubts. Sometimes it's hard to know what's expected of you.

"I think I know enough to keep from killing myself. Now the other people out there might be in some deep shit." He laughed and began to paddle toward the back of the cove.

Ahead of him a gar or carp—one of the stupid breeds of fish that is always in the way—broke the surface of the water and disappeared under one of the plane's pontoons. Dalton stroked some more, then spun the plane until it faced the lake. He climbed in and bumped the starter. The prop kicked into gear. I gave the sign when all the skiers were heading the other direction. More wind that twisted the leaves on the trees. More waves. Both of our docks rocked in the huge wake. Then Dalton was gone on his own, and I wished there was a way I could warn the rest of the world to watch the sky.

That morning, during his solo flight, Dalton started something that became the ritual. He buzzed my house. Buzzed his, too, as a matter of fact. Our houses were so close together that you couldn't really dive-bomb one with a seaplane without rattling the windows in the other. He never attacked right after takeoff. He would play around in the sky for an hour or so, then he would show up over our cove.

You could hear him coming a couple of minutes away. A thin hum somewhere through the trees. The hum grew louder and more frantic. Then the plane would appear a few hundred feet above the houses, closing quickly. He would dive at a harsh angle, then pull the nose up when he was about to gain too much speed to avoid the treetops, just when he was about out of control. As he pulled up from the dive, he always leaned from the cockpit and threw something at my house. Always something different. One of his sneakers, a boat cushion, fishing tackle. Once, a real fish.

Later, when he had tied the boat to the dock, he would run across the bridge into my yard and yell, "How close was I?"

He kept it up, week after week. The buzzing and the throwing. I couldn't enjoy any of my Saturday mornings because of the anticipation. I couldn't eat breakfast. I couldn't grade history papers. I had been by myself so long that I had come to appreciate the qualities of silence, but Dalton and his plane were ruining things. I would pace back and forth inside the house, avoiding the back porch and the yard and especially the sky. I was being held hostage by the fact that it was probably going to happen again, and I couldn't do anything to stop it.

The earliest sound of the plane's engine would always fool me. I'd trick myself into thinking it was a confused bottlefly trapped between the window and the screen. Or maybe it was the ceiling fan in the living room that needed a squirt of oil for its squeak. Then I would recall the takeoff.

I'd remember it was Saturday. It was Dalton in his goddamn plane. And he was doing it again, trying to get a reaction from me.

I would get madder and madder, wasting time, waiting to be positive it was him. I'd watch the sky, trying to pinpoint the noise, and I would finally see the yellow pontoons and the red stripes and the little drift of exhaust when he backed off of the throttle for his dive. It was then that I would leave my house, walk into the yard (through the weeds, if it was spring or summer), cross the bridge and shake my head at him as he thundered away. As he began to gain altitude above the lake, I would cross the bridge, go through Dalton's front door and make love to his daughter in her father's bed.

I have no excuses. There is no motivation I can put my finger on. Dalton wanted a reaction, and by God, I was going to give it to him.

It was always the quietest thing you have ever heard between two people. Raleigh never made the slightest sound. She pretty much accepted me with a narrow-eyed indifference that reminded me of a tired, underpaid prostitute. She rarely talked, which is no surprise.

Once she called me "definitely one of Pavlov's best dogs," and I suppose she had a point. When I heard the plane, when I confirmed that it was Dalton, I couldn't wait to get back at him in the worst way I could imagine. In my own way, I salivated.

I didn't start off with revenge in mind. In fact, the first time I crossed the bridge during the buzz-over, I simply went to ask Raleigh if she would tell her father not to fly so near the houses. I told her it might sound trivial, but I couldn't get anything done because I was waiting to be interrupted. Saturday, I told her, was the only day I could truly enjoy, and her father was destroying it.

"I'm sorry to have to ask you to do my dirty work for me," I said, "but I've already said something to him, and he just laughs. It's been driving me crazy for months. I guess I thought maybe he would get bored and stop."

Raleigh didn't answer for maybe half a minute. I started to back down the steps.

"He doesn't listen to me either," she said finally. "But we have this understanding."

She turned and walked out of the room. I stood in the open doorway for a minute, trying to decide what she meant by "an understanding," and I laughed out loud at the fact that when Raleigh finally decides to say things to me, I have no idea what in the hell she's talking about.

The next Saturday, Dalton asked me again to help with his takeoff. I started to refuse, but if I did, he could kill someone on takeoff, and I would feel like it was my fault. All I needed was a death on my hands. Dalton didn't say a word about his flight plans and neither did I as he pushed toward the rear of the cove.

I spent the morning walking from room to room in my house, waiting to see what would happen. I was hopeful that Raleigh had spoken with him. Suddenly, it was there. The bottlefly. The squeaky fan. The plane.

I ran next door in full view. Dalton, I supposed, would think I was going to wait for his triumphant arrival at the dock, where I would toss him a rope and reel him and his plane in. It was hot out, I remember. I ran through the Sorrel and Oxalis, kicking up spores and pollen that stuck to my legs as I went by. I heard something thud in the yard behind me. Dalton's missile. It looked like something he'd taken out of the freezer. Raleigh was already at the door.

"I've had enough of your father," I said, a little out of breath.

She nodded, I think, and walked down the hall then turned into Dalton's bedroom. I could hear music coming from inside, and as I got closer, the music grew softer, which I thought was strange until I realized that a record was finishing and fading. Even silent, the fancy stereo system in Dalton's room was lit like a science project. It was dark in his room, and I knew exactly what was happening.

I didn't know why. In fact, I remember thinking that the reasons weren't important at this point. What was important was whether or not to fall into this with Raleigh. The simple answers. A yes or a no. That's what was important right then.

I turned back toward the hall to leave and Raleigh said too loudly, "It's always twenty-five minutes or so before he gets back to the dock. In twenty-five minutes, we can both fuck him over."

I sat on the bed to help her off with her T-shirt, but she stopped me and said, "Would you go turn that record over?"

I knew then that no matter what I decided to do, Raleigh would always have something else on her mind.

Every time I was with Raleigh, I thought about history. I could have thought about her, but I could never see very well in the room. I could only feel the long hair that had never been cut and the skin that was toughened from all of the sun. But history always seemed to take over and fill my head. In fact, history was never more clear than when I was with her, surrounded by the darkness and the stereo lights and the whine of Dalton's fast-fading airshow. I thought about Pilgrims and patriots and Lizzie Borden. I was still the autopilot even there, in the bedroom.

And it was very easy to think during our sessions. Raleigh never made any sort of noise. There was only the muffled sound of the stereo. At one point I decided I was definitely insane for letting the sound of a plane drive me into bed with a teenager. So I tried to stop. I tried to give myself things to do on Saturday mornings that were so vital, so unavoidable, I couldn't possibly run across that bridge. But then came the engine noise, and I suddenly found myself adjusting a stereo in the dark and thinking about history. I told myself that men had done stranger things for less, that throughout history, men had been immoral for sillier reasons. I could validate anything.

I felt better.

Other than our twenty-five minutes once a week, nothing changed between us neighbors. Raleigh never spoke to me. Dalton and I sat on the dock and drank beer and fed the fish. I didn't look him in the eye. We discussed the water level in the cove and where Raleigh should go to school after she graduated. When winter came, we scouted out dead hardwoods on Dalton's property and cut them for firewood. I cruised through another year at Crescent, skipping the Lizzie Borden saga as some sort of private tribute to Raleigh. I would see her occasionally in the hall, her head inside a locker, but it was business as usual. And every Saturday, Dalton took to the skies.

Saturdays were holy days for Dalton, I thought. It never rained on a Saturday that whole year. There were always bright and crisp skies, maybe a high swatch of clouds. It was never foggy or threatening. The lake was always the same brilliant blue as the sky. It was always perfect flying weather, and Dalton always flew. Then as suddenly as the plane had appeared a couple of years earlier, it was gone. It was early in the spring. I remember that the weeds were beginning to show themselves. One morning in the middle of that week, Shaker showed up again, hiding behind his glasses. I watched from my kitchen window while I drank coffee. This time, Shaker gave Dalton some money and a pat on the back, and Shaker flew away in the plane without even checking for boats in his path.

Dalton stood on the dock, rocking in the plane's wake. I was too far away to guess what was going on. I had no idea that Dalton had just sold his plane. The following Saturday, the plane was still gone, and it rained like a bitch the whole weekend.

"When I was up there, I could see everything I owned," Dalton said, pointing at the sky. "Now we have to go down. I still own things there, too."

Down meant underwater. It meant scuba diving.

With the money he had from the plane sale, he
bought scuba gear for the both of us.

"I don't know how to work this equipment,"
I said.

"So? I didn't know how to fly until somebody
showed me. I'm going to show you how to dive."

His plan this time was to find his old house, the
one he grew up in. He said he wanted to sit on the
porch where he discovered his father dead. I thought
that was a sick idea, and I told him so. He just answered, "It's not sick. It's just different."

Even though he talked me into going, I was trying
to avoid him as much as possible. Sometimes I decided he sold the plane because he found out about
my in-flight visits to his room. The thought of this
made me catch my breath. It kept me awake nights.
Sometimes I decided it was just a matter of timing, of
coincidence. A matter of history and the logical flow
of events.

Dalton told me he sold it because it wasn't fun
anymore. He never said a word about Raleigh. And
Raleigh, she just went on like normal. Silent and
thoughtful, on the verge of saying something either
profound or confusing. There were, of course, no
more Saturdays, no more adjustments to the stereo.
No more twenty-five minutes. There was no need.

We practiced first in the shallow end of our cove.
Dalton read a thin library book on scuba diving, then
showed me how to breathe through the regulator.
And how to clear the hose. How to read the gauges.
We practiced swimming with the tanks on. We even
practiced emergency breathing through a single
regulator. We moved into deeper and deeper water,
until he said we were ready to hunt for his house.

Dalton knew roughly where it should be, though
he admitted that with eighty feet or so of water over
it, the house was going to be hard to find. "Everything looks so different now. I'm used to the coves
and beaches," he said as we paddled his aluminum
john boat toward the mouth of the cove. There was
a slight chop on the surface, a little breeze from the
south, but the water seemed warm for that time of

year.

Dalton peered into his reflection over the side every once in awhile, looking I suppose, for his roof or the top of a chimney. He stopped paddling and began to study the shore, scouting for landmarks.

"There was this one tree on a little hill," he said. "You always noticed it from our porch." He looked from both sides of the boat, then shook his head.

"Why don't we just try to get in the general neighborhood and look around underwater?" I asked. "You know, it might take a few tries. We might not find anything today."

I paddled, and he watched for another half hour. He directed me with hand signals from his seat in the front of the boat.

Finally, he turned around. "I think we're close," he said and began to lift the scuba gear onto his shoulders. We had what I guessed were the necessities: tanks, regulators, fins, masks. And we each had a flashlight plus a kind of underwater chalkboard, in case we wanted to be specific about something we saw.

We didn't have an anchor, but it didn't matter. The water was too deep. Dalton said we should just let the boat drift to shore in the breeze, and we could swim for it later when we had finished. He slid out of the boat first. I fell off right behind him, and the two of us sank through a cloud of bubbles, down to where the light was thin and gray like dusk.

There are a hundred stories about what was left behind when the dam was built and the lake filled up. Tiny crossroads communities, houses, mills—all still standing. You'd expect that kind of thing, I guess. But there was always talk about what didn't escape. Animals that were somehow caught in the creeping flood. Hundreds of graves that relatives couldn't afford to move to higher ground. Supposedly, there were even skeletons of stubborn farmers who refused to leave and let the water cover them in their sleep. You never think about these things until there's a chance you might discover the remains. Once I was underwater, I couldn't help but wonder about what I might find with a kick or two of my fins. But all I saw were a few schools of bream and a lazy largemouth bass as we angled in the direction of the bottom.

Dalton came to a quick stop. We were probably ten feet off the bottom, but the water was too murky to be sure about anything. He pointed, and ahead of us, anchored in the mud and silt and shimmering in the invisible currents, was the outline of a house. I saw a pair of chimneys and could even make out the huge porch that wrapped around the front. I expected the house to look like a shipwreck, maybe listing to one side, covered with crust and full of creatures. But it looked almost content, almost like it enjoyed the quiet of the lake bottom, and from where we floated, you could tell that the house had been white at one time. You could see windows that still had their glass. You could see the pillars of the front porch. Dalton's eyes were big inside his mask. He grinned around his regulator.

He took off for the house, and I pulled in behind him. His flippers slapped me in the mask several times, almost knocked it off my face, so I backed away. The closer we swam, the more you could tell the house had been taken over by the lake. There was a thin, even coat of algae covering the paint. The muck of the bottom had piled high against one of the outside walls like a brown snowdrift, almost up to the window sills. Fish darted in and out of strange holes in the siding and under the porch. Under the eaves, several bird's nests of heavy fishing line and an assortment of hooks and lost lures shimmied in the current. The house was still standing. It was still strong, but the lake was going to win one day.

Dalton floated toward the front door. It was locked or stuck. He scrambled around the side for the back door. He put a flipper against the outside wall, and with both hands, pulled the door away from its frame. We entered and swam toward the open space, and we both hit the wall that suddenly appeared. Dalton made a signal to use the flashlights, and we followed the dim beam of light and bubbles into the kitchen and then down the hall. The house was empty and the walls seemed brown and greasy. A huge striped bass swam through the beam of my light, and I sucked too hard on the regulator. It felt like I was coughing through my ears. I stopped for a second to clear my head, then continued on in the direction of Dalton's light. Near the front door, Dalton snatched his board and scribbled with his marker.

THIS IS SHIT.
THERE'S NOTHING HERE.

He underlined "nothing." He was mad. I guess he wanted there to be furniture and lamps in all of the rooms. He seemed to be looking for something and was down another hall and gone with a couple of quick kicks. Even with my flashlight, I lost him in the dark. I couldn't find his trail of bubbles. I kept running up against walls and door jambs that appeared to move when I hit them. I had been to this house a couple of times when Dalton's father was alive, but I couldn't remember the layout now. That was too long ago.

I found a stairway and swam up the bannister, still searching for a sign of Dalton. Nothing. No bubbles, no evidence that he had scraped against the wall and rubbed the algae off. I felt like I was in the worst kind of funhouse, one without mirrors and the only sound the steady breath in my ears. I looked in every room I discovered. I checked my watch, which said I only had a few minutes of air left. Dalton, I decided, had already headed for the surface. He'd probably been doing the same thing, looking for me. He probably had the boat now, paddling to a spot above my head. It was a waste of time to go down the stairs just so I could swim up to the surface, so I found a big window over the front porch that was rotting in its frame. I pushed the glass and wood away and let myself out.

With a couple of kicks I was yards above the house. I could look down on the roof. I could see the outline of the porch. I was flying. I was hovering above the chimney like a strange sort of plane. If I

had wanted, I could've dive-bombed the house.
I stayed there, looking down, and I knew why Dalton
loved to fly. He only wanted a different view of things.
He wanted to see some of what he had made.

I drifted there, my arms out like wings, flaps on
my feet, and I knew that the only reason he had
stopped flying was because he found out about me
and Raleigh. Nothing else would have made him give
up the view from the air. At that precise second, I lost
all of my doubts. Dalton knew, had probably known
for a while, and I hadn't told him. I started to get
sick, and there had been nothing in Dalton's scuba
diving book about that problem.

Dalton drowned in the huge attic. He had slith-
ered through a small trap door in one of the upstairs
hall closets and couldn't find his way out again before
his tanks emptied. When the divers from the Rescue
Squad found him, they said he was tangled among the
roof joists of his father's house, his tanks and weight
belt discarded and scattered on the attic floor.

I kept waiting for them to tell me that his chalkboard was clutched in his hand, that he had written
something about his daughter and his neighbor,
something I would have to carry around for the rest of
my life like a disease. Or maybe I was hoping for a
sign of forgiveness, some sort of underwater Bible
verse that would make me feel better. But Dalton's
slate was clean, and that, I know now, was the worst
thing that could have happened—not knowing what
he thought of me when he died.

After his funeral, Raleigh left for college without
saying a word to me. She forgot to turn out one light
in the house, somewhere in a back hallway, and it
burned for months until one evening I noticed it had
finally gone out. Dalton's house has been perfectly
dark for years.

It was me and the shoreline and the shell of a
house next door. And there were the weeds. Every
spring, just as school was about to let out, just as the
autopilot was about to come in for a landing, the

weeds started. I chopped and hoed. I sprayed, but still they came. They wouldn't let me forget the history I had. I finally gave up, except for my little revolt in the middle of the night, my short ride to the cemetery and Dalton's grave. But even that lost any clear purpose.   Now, I just seem to move along on some current, happy enough with what I have.

On Deno Trakas

by Shelby Hearon

I SAVOR THE SHORT STORIES OF DENO
TRAKAS BECAUSE I KNOW I'M GUARANTEED
GOOD TALK. PERHAPS BECAUSE HE WAS RAISED IN A
family of musicians, or perhaps because he began as
a poet, weighing each word for sense and sound,
Deno has that most valuable of gifts for a fiction
writer: a good ear. I know, reading him, I will hear
real voices, speaking of matters that matter, revealing
most while trying to conceal, speaking of what
mustn't be spoken.

   Talk in stories is often called "dialogue," but to me
that term conveys a two-way attempt to debate, to
explore, to make things clear. Where good talk in
fiction, like talk in everyday life, does nothing to make

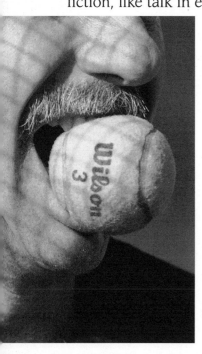

matters clear and seldom settles
anything. Yet Deno with his fine-
tuned ear picks up the oblique
emotion and the swift piercing
word in what his people say or
almost say to each other.

   Take the stories included
here. In "Eugene," a white
lawyer and lunch-time basketball
player invites a fellow player, a
black TV cameraman, to dinner.
I see them walk across the white
man's fresh-cut fescue lawn,
through the white pine and
dogwood, into his heavily mort-
gaged home, and I listen to what
they say. And when the guest
asks his host right out at the
table, "How much money do you

make?" I know the lawyer will lie, and he does. And I know he will think: "He couldn't have asked a more personal question if he'd asked me about my sex life."

In "The Philosopher's Landlord," a professor new to the area, sipping sweetened Southern tea, agrees to act as a marriage counselor between the landlord and his cheating wife. And I know that when the philosopher asks, "Do you still love your wife?" the real question is, does the professor love his girlfriend with the long legs and the pretty hair? And how do you tell?

In "The Center of the Universe," an English teacher and sometimes-writer is helping his teenage daughter invent a short story to bring up her failing grade. When she suggests that maybe her girl gets kidnapped at the mall and the daddy asks, "Who would want her?" I know that he will have to follow her to see his deepest fear realized: his daughter kidnapped before his very eyes by a short boy with wandering hands and cigarette breath. I also know the seemingly casual, offhand talk of all the stories will present in the sum of the words the writer's central view of men and women: The man will always come in second; the woman will always prefer something or someone else first.

The black man in the story about the ballplayers says of the expensive house and grounds, "You've got a pretty picture here, with a lot of frame around it, a lot of protection." This serves as a metaphor for all the people in these stories—and, of course, for all of us as well. The talent of Deno Trakas's pure pitch is that—whether under the "golden pond of a South Carolina sunset," or on a "polished silver May morning"—as his people talk, their words tear away the frame. At least for an instant, the protection is gone, and we see the beating hearts and bare faces behind the facade.

And the good talk remains in our hearts like an overheard conversation.

—*Shelby Hearon, a native of Kentucky, is the author of fourteen novels, including* Owning Jolene, *winner of an American Academy of Arts and Letters Literature Award. She now makes her home in Burlington, Vermont.*

Eugene

Blank dribbles through the middle and flips the ball up, over the slashing arm of the opposing center—it kisses high on the board and drops through: the game is over, we won 11-8, Shakey, G, Blank, Smoke and I. I'm feeling pretty good because I made two baskets, played hard D, and didn't turn the ball over. We slap hands and saunter off the court, through the double doors and down the hall to get some water at the fountain before the next game. I've got time for one more before I have to shower, grab a burger and get back to the office. About half the guys are like me, lawyers, insurance men, or salesmen squeezing in an hour of ball at lunchtime here at the Y, while the other half are third-shift workers at Drayton, or night watchmen, or bus drivers, or between jobs. Most of us are regulars and know each other on the court—we know the money players, the ice cream shooters, the deft passers.

"Keep shootin, Rob," G says as we head back inside. I nod. He knows I'm a reluctant shooter, more likely to pass than take the J, especially if I've missed one or two. So he's speaking his faith to keep me loose. We go to the far end of the court to shoot and stay warm while some of the guys who were waiting shoot from the yellow line to see who will play us. Smoke and G joke around, and I miss the conversation except for G saying, "Yeah, so how come you never invite me to your house, Smoke?" G takes a shot, left handed, high arch, nothing but net. I catch it and sling it back to him.

"You too ugly. I don't want to scare the kids," Smoke says, grinning.

"See? Why you always dissen me?"

G's got a point. He's not one to joke by ridicule, and he's not ugly. Not exactly handsome, but not ugly. About 5'9", 165, oval face, complexion like stale milk chocolate, hair long in back, ringlets dripping down his neck. I like to be on his team because even though he's a good shooter, from outside or driving the lane, he's a team player, unselfish, scrappy, runs the floor, presses, never gets winded. He takes another shot. Bottom.

"You can come to my house," I say as I throw the ball to him again. As soon as the words are out I wonder why I said them—I like G, respect him, and am happy to be on a winning team with him, but I don't really know him, and to have him over would be weird. I'm afraid I'd be embarrassed because I have a big house, bigger than I can afford, and even though it's a mess inside, just the size of it is ostentatious—I don't want him to think I'm a spoiled rich kid, because I'm not. I wait to see if he's going to take me seriously. Shakey and Blank begin to drift our way, so we ought to be starting up in a few minutes—

"See now? This white man, I don't even know where he live, but he invite me over. So what kind of friend does that make you, Smoke?" G pouts his lips when he says "you."

Smoke says, "He been watching too many movies. You been checking out 'White Men Can't Jump,' Rob?"

"Yeah, I watch it every morning while I eat biscuits and grits. My kids love it."

G laughs, Ha, and drives in, going right over the top of Smoke for emphasis. I get the rebound and take the ball to the wing, bank one off the glass. Smoke fires it back out to me and says, "Rob's one of those liberals. I bet he works for Habitat and smokes marijuana."

I shoot again and miss. "Yeah, but not at the same time."

G shouts down to the other end of the floor, "Come on, let's play." Five guys peel their shirts off and stalk toward us, including Bobby who played pro ball for the CBA before the league folded. We'll have our hands full.

When G guns his '90 Celica up my long driveway, my son and I are there shooting baskets at the goal that I put in right after we bought the house last year. He pulls off into the new grass where I recently overseeded, so as not to encroach on our court. I toss the ball to my son and go over to greet G as he gets out. "Welcome," I say and shake his hand, a normal handshake. "You have any trouble finding us?"

"No, except you said you had a big house, you didn't say nothing about no mansion. How many kids you got, ten or twenty?"

"Just two."

"Whew. This some place." Together we turn and survey my property, a 3,500-square-foot white, two-story colonial house set on a hill in a mostly white neighborhood called Silver Maple Estates, named of course for the silver maples that dominate the view— I have nine in my yard, along with almost as many oaks, some elms, hickory, sycamore, white pines, lots of dogwoods. The leaves are beginning to turn for the season, the fresh-cut fescue lawn is dark green—on a golden afternoon like this one, a year ago, my wife showed me the house for the first time and began to convince me that we should overextend ourselves to get it.

"Yeah, it's a pain to take care of though. I get BJ to cut the front yard for me. BJ, come here."

My eight-year-old dribbles over to us. "This is G."

"Hey little man," G says and holds out his hand, palm up. BJ gives him five. "You gonna be a ball player like your dad?"

"Yeah. I can already make it from the three point line. Watch." We have no three-point line on the driveway, but he dribbles to the edge of the carport just behind my wife's car and launches the ball on the run from his hip. It bounces off the rim and he scampers after it. "I've made it before, though."

"I'm sure you have. That's a pretty good shot."

"Let G take a shot," I say, and BJ throws him the ball.

G dips it with both hands deep behind his head to stretch, then bounces it and bends his knees a couple of times. "I didn't know we were going to play ball or I'd brought my clothes." He's wearing a pressed, long-sleeve white shirt, pleated gray and black slacks, and loafers, even though I told him I'd probably be wearing jeans and am. He shoots, the high arch I've seen so many times. I want it to go in but it's just short—he hasn't adjusted for the slope of the drive-way.

"I ought to take you on now," I say, "before you're warmed up and while I have the home court advantage—maybe I could beat you for once."

"Shoot, you beat me plenty."

I appreciate the lie, pat him on the shoulder and say, "Let's go on in and see if supper's ready."

We walk between the '84 Mazda and the '86 van and enter the family room from the carport. Like most of the house, the room is minimally furnished, and its pieces are poorly mismatched: a blue-gray carpet, brown and white print contemporary sofa, beige recliner, a coffee table with an old nineteen-inch color TV, rabbit ear antenna sticking out because we don't have an antenna on the roof and we don't have cable. Over the mantel hangs a charcoal picture of a horse, drawn by my sister, the only real art in the house. I'm conscious of the musty smell of the carpet, which makes me think of an old TV show, "All in the Family" or something, in which a couple of black guys broke into a white family's house and commented that all white people's houses smelled funny.

"Nice place," G says, looking around.

"Thanks. We haven't fixed it up on the inside. We spent all our money, and then some, just to buy the place."

"How much a place like this cost?"

I don't want to answer, but I don't want to embarrass him for asking a rude question. "A hundred fifty thousand," I say, rounding down the purchase price a few thousand and not counting the bedroom suite we added, which was another fifty, which, by itself was more than our first house.

He whistles. "But you don't get no cable?"

"Can't afford it after I pay the mortgage," I say, smiling, but not really joking.

"I got me a satellite dish, work pretty good, but need a new chip. Man says it'll cost $200."

I nod. "Sounds like a lot."

"Yeah."

"Come on in. You hungry?"

"I'm always hungry."

We walk into the kitchen, which, with its open space, light, and plentiful cabinets, was the room to first enchant my wife. She's cutting some of my home-grown tomatoes for the salad when we come in. "Laura, this is G."

She turns, puts down her knife, dries her hands on a dish towel, and shakes his hand. "It's nice to meet you, G."

"Nice to meet *you*," he says. "Nice of you to have me over."

"I hope you like spaghetti," I say, lifting the lid on the sauce and stirring. We thought hard about what to have, whether to go ethnic/exotic, or expensive/fancy, or simple. We decided on simple ethnic, but I wasn't confident of the decision.

"Sure."

"I wanted to grill steaks, but we don't have a grill. We have a natural gas line all ready to hook up, but I just haven't had a chance to buy a grill yet."

"Man, you got to stop apologizing for being poor. You living like a *king*, grill or no damn grill."

"Tell him, G," my wife adds, nodding my way, and resuming her chopping.

Laura and I, like most couples, have conflicting views on money—she's a spender, I'm a hoarder—and we argue often over sums great and small. The house has been the greatest of our battles, and a year after the closing, I'm still pissed that I surrendered. "OK, sorry, no more apologies. How about something to drink, G. I've got beer, wine, iced tea, Coke . . ."

"You got some red wine? I like wine with spaghetti."

"You got it. Laura, you want some?"

"I'll have a little. Where do you live, G?"

"I stay in a little place on Thomas Street, over
behind the college."

"That's a nice neighborhood. When I was in
school I used to ride my bike through there on the
way to the shopping center."

"Yeah, it's pretty nice except the college trying to
buy it out, the college and the hospital coming from
the other direction."

"Really? What does the college want it for?" I
hand him his wine.

"Hell if I know. They always wanting to build
some new damn thing, tennis courts, or football
stadium or something. My landlord tell me he'll sell
in a minute if the price right."

This is a new perspective for me, a contributor to
the college's athletic program. "Where will you move
if he does?"

"I don't know. Not many nice cheap neighbor-
hoods left. Seem like if it's cheap it's full of crack."

Laura interrupts, "Rob, if you'll get the bread out
of the oven, I think we'll be ready to eat."

"I'll go get your boy," G offers.

"Good, thanks."

I put the garlic bread in a basket and take it to the
dining room table, which Laura has set with good
china and sterling silver, although I argued for everyday. She brings in the salad. "What do you think?"
I ask.

"Everything's fine. Relax."

When I came home a week ago and said, "Guess
who's coming to dinner?" she asked who and then
why. G, and I don't know why, I said honestly. It
came up, and I just felt like it, G's my friend, and I've
never invited a black person to my house . . . and it'll
be good for the kids to see us socialize with a black
man. She wondered, I think, if there were some other
motive or agenda, but she didn't press me; she just
asked what we'd fix and when. Since then, I won-

dered myself why I did it. I asked some of my friends if they'd ever had a black person over to dinner, and they all said no. I didn't think the reason was prejudice. We were all fairly liberal, we'd gone to high school in the seventies, after integration, and those of us who'd played basketball or football in school had spent lots of time in integrated company. But I finally decided the question of my own segregation had a simple answer—I didn't socialize with blacks because I didn't socialize much with anybody, only a few close friends from work, and they happened to be white.

I send BJ to the bathroom to wash his hands, then we all sit down in the dining room, at the big cherry table that matches the cherry china cabinet, our nicest furniture. "I'm sorry my daughter isn't here, too," I say, "but her soccer coach called a practice at the last minute."

"How old's she?"

"Twelve."

"I got a five-year-old boy, live with his mama in New York. I don't get to see him much. But I send him lot of clothes and stuff. I sent him some Pumps."

I'm thinking that BJ wanted some Pumps but I flatly refused because they cost too much when Laura asks, "Will you say grace, Rob?"

"BJ, you do it."

"OK." We bow our heads. "ABCD gold fish."

"Not that one," I say as he giggles.

"God is great, God is good, let us thank him for our food, amen."

From the head of the table, I heap spaghetti on plates and pass them around. Laura hands the salad bowl to G and says, "I've got a bag full of BJ's old clothes I was going to give to Goodwill. You're welcome to them, G."

I look up, worried that he might be offended by the handout. "That'd be good," he says as he smothers his spaghetti with meat sauce.

"What does G stand for?" BJ asks.

I wonder if the question is too personal, but G answers without hesitation. "Gene, grand, and good looking," he says and adds a drift of Parmesan cheese—the real kind for a change, not that dust in the green can—to the mound on his plate. "What does BJ stand for?"

"Bob Junior."

"Bound, Jumper."

"Yeah," my son assents.

"Did you play ball in school, G?" I ask the question generically, not knowing whether he went to college.

"In high school, up north."

"How long've you been in South Carolina?"

"About ten years. I used to work with Spike Lee. You know who he is?"

"The movie director?"

"Yeah, that's my man. I helped him with 'She's Gotta Have It,' but then people started giving him all this money and he decided to move to Hollywood. He ask me did I want to go, but I said nah. I couldn't see me hanging with all those rich white folks on Rodeo Boulevard. Maybe I shoulda gone, maybe I'd been in 'White Men' instead of Wesley Snipes. Ha," he laughed his one-syllable laugh.

"That's amazing. Do you still hear from him?"

"Yeah, he call every so often. Last year I went to Atlanta to see him when he was making that movie there."

"What do you do now? I'm sorry I don't know."

"I'm a cameraman for channel seven."

"No kidding. Do you like it?"

"It's all right. You a lawyer, right?"

"Yeah."

"You like it?"

"It's all right."

"How much money you make?"

Again, I hesitate. He couldn't have asked a more personal question if he'd asked about my sex life. I don't discuss my income with anybody—I even do my own taxes—except to fight about it with Laura, who is looking at me with a curious grin. I answer, "About sixty thousand," a low estimate, not including investment income.

"So you not one of those high rollers like Vic."

Vic is another lawyer who plays ball with us occasionally, drives a Lexus, lives in a million-dollar house on the west side. "No, I'm not in the same league with Vic."

"How'd he make all that money?"

"Well, his wife's family has money for one thing, and he's chased a few ambulances in his time, gotten some big settlements."

"You work, Laura?"

"Part time, as a dental technician."

"How much you make?"

"Sixteen thousand," she says flat out, showing that she's not embarrassed.

G nods, and left-handed forks and twirls a little bale of spaghetti and gets it to his mouth without splattering any sauce on his white shirt, which is better than I'm doing, eating without paying attention, collecting stains. I'm glad we've finished the discussion of money, and I'm thinking of what to change the subject to when he says, "So you two bring home about $4500 a month."

I'm startled, he's so close. Laura raises her eyes at me and answers, "Yes, that's good figuring."

"And mortgage, insurance and taxes run about 1500."

He's about 500 low because I didn't tell him the true value of the house with the addition, but I say, "About that."

BJ has never heard us talk about our salaries and expenses at the table and seems fascinated, staring at G, then at me and Laura while he plays with his food. I've had enough and say, "Look G, I'm not comfortable talking about my finances."

"Just trying to have a conversation. What you want to talk about, Rob?"

"I don't know."

"How about the Braves? You think they can win the series?"

"I do," BJ shouts.

"What do you talk about when you're with your other friends?" I ask.

"You mean, what do black people talk about?"

"That's not what I meant, but yeah, what do black people talk about? Is it any different from what white people talk about?"

"I guess it all depend on which black people you talking to. Me and my friends we don't talk about mutual funds and shit like that. Excuse me, little man."

"It's OK. My dad says shit too."

"Ha," G laughs. "But we talk about money all the time. And sports. And we talk about our girlfriends and our wives when they hassling us. You know."

"Yeah, I know all about wives hassling you," I say, relieved that the conversation has lightened up.

Laura, naturally, defends her gender. "And I bet your women talk about their men hassling them."

"They sure do."

"So, we're not so different after all," I say.

"I didn't say *that*. You got your white mansion here in your white hood—I bet they not a black family in the whole zip code. You got two salaries, you got two cars paid for, you got insurance and investments—you got a pretty picture here with lot of frame around it, lot of protection. That the difference. They not but a handful black people in this town got what you got. Forty-five percent living below poverty level, a step away from nothing. This sure is good spaghetti. Salad good too."

"Thank you," Laura says. "We've got some apple pie and ice cream for dessert."

"I can smell it cooking."

Laura gets up to check on the pie. "So what's the answer, G?"

"Answer to what?"

"To the financial inequality."

"I don't know no answer, except you give us your money."

"That's what taxes and welfare are for."

"Now don't get me started on that."

"Do you need money?" I ask.

"I always need money."

"How much?"

"Why?" He stops eating and looks up at me. "You

gonna give me some?"

Suddenly I realize what I've done—I've insulted him, and now I've cornered myself. "I could loan you some."

He shakes his head, finishes off his wine while he thinks. "OK."

"OK what?"

"Give me some money. Give me two hundred dollars."

BJ looks at me wide-eyed, as if to say, uh-oh, now what are you going to do, Dad?

"I'd have to write you a check."

"I've seen one before."

He doesn't move except to put his hands on the arms of the chair and lean back. So I get up right then to find my checkbook. When I pass through the kitchen Laura whispers, "What are you doing?"

"I don't know," I say. When I get back to the table with my checkbook, G is talking to BJ about allowance. "How should I make it out?" I ask.

"Eugene Sommers." G pushes the last bite of spaghetti onto his fork with a piece of bread.

I tear it off and hand it to him. He glances at it, folds it in half, and puts it in his shirt pocket. "Thanks."

"You're welcome." I want to ask him what he's going to do with it and when I can expect to get it back, but the whole thing—money talk and money changing hands—makes my chest tight, so I gulp down the rest of my wine and divert my attention to finishing my food.

Mercifully, Laura comes in and asks, "Who's ready for dessert?"

I don't go to the Y the next day and tell myself it's because I have a lot of work to do, which is always true, but the real reason is that I don't want to see G. Not that anything else happened—we ate to overcome our discomfort, a whole pie and almost a half gallon of Breyer's vanilla, and then G took his leave, saying he had to be at the studio at 9:00.

All day I feel pressed and edgy. Everyone seems to

be in my face, and I keep stepping back when I'm
standing with someone in conversation. I don't feel
like talking on the phone either and have my secretary
hold my calls all afternoon, saying that I'm in court.
I feel like I'm in court, a victim. And it's all because
of that $200, which I'm sure I'll never see again. But
it's not just the money—I *can* afford a $200 loss after
all—it's the feeling of being taken advantage of. I
don't like it one damn bit.

When I get home, there's a big box in my spot in
the carport. I'm pissed at BJ for dragging it from
wherever and blocking my way, but when I get up to
it I see that it's not empty—it's filled with a new
natural gas grill, a nice one. I've been out pricing
them and know this one runs about $400 at Home
Depot. At first I think, why would Laura go out and
get one now? And then I think, G. Inside, Laura
confirms that she had nothing to do with it. I look up
Eugene Sommers in the phone book, but no one
answers my call.

I go to the Y earlier than usual the next day, not
early enough to make the first game, but I'll have the
ride for the next. While I'm shooting on the side court
to warm up, G comes in. Perfect, we'll be on the same
team, and if a good big man walks through the door,
we might have a good run. Grinning like a fool, I
wave him over and go to meet him. "What's up,
Rob?" he says and shakes my hand.

I pull him to me and throw my arm around his
shoulders. "That was the nicest thing anybody's done
for me in a long time, G. But I can't accept it."

"Why not?" He takes the ball from me and shoots,
misses. We wander toward the basket.

"It's too much. I know how much those things
cost."

"I put it on plastic, don't hurt a bit."

"But the grill is twice as much as the check."

"I didn't buy the grill with the check. The grill a
present." He scoops the ball up, dribbles out to the
wing, and pops one in.

I catch the ball on first bounce. "What are you
saying? You mean you're giving me a grill, and you're

going to pay me back $200?" I stand there, holding the ball.

"Give me my change," he says, meaning give him another shot. I throw him the ball. "You *want* me to pay it back?" he asks.

"No, I want to pay *you* back. I owe you two hundred dollars."

He sinks another one. "You got to ease up, Rob. You all nervous because you trying to make it come out even, but it won't. It don't ever come out even." I throw him the ball, he takes a quick step to his left and shoots again, bottom. I hit him again.

"So what am I supposed to do?" I ask.

"Grill steak next time."

The Philosopher's Landlord

My landlord was asleep on my couch, half bundled in a down parka, snoring coarsely. I didn't wake him—I have always had a deep respect for sleep—I just padded as quietly as possible in my socks through the living room, staying close to the walls so as not to hit the creaks in the wood floor, on my way to the bathroom. School had just gotten out for the year, so I was blessed with leisure, had nothing to do but get started on my summer project of trying to revise my dissertation on Kant into a publishable book, an onerous task that I was in no hurry to tackle. Besides, my landlord was an agreeable man, always came over within a couple of days whenever I called to report a problem, usually fixed the problem himself (although he was surprisingly clumsy with tools), sometimes chatted in his slow, self-conscious way, and never reprimanded me if the rent was a few days late, or a week. I assumed he had a good reason for letting himself in and sleeping on my couch, and he'd explain, of course, when he got up. I was just glad Tess hadn't spent the night—she would have found his presence strange and disconcerting.

After my shower, I went to the kitchen and started the coffee, then went out the back door and walked around the house to retrieve the newspaper. When I returned, he was sitting at the kitchen table, a middle-age country man with a small chin, big ears, wild eyebrows, tame, thin brown hair, and thick arms strapped across his barrel chest, sitting there looking at me.

"Mornin, Philosopher."

"Good morning, Landlord." We had always called each other by our professions—he started it—he seemed to like having a philosophy professor as a tenant. I handed him the newspaper. "I'm going to make toast—would you like some?"

"All right." In his Southern accent, the words sounded like awe plus rye with a t. He opened the paper and started to read while I prepared breakfast, wondering what had brought him here after midnight, the hour I had gone to bed, and whether he would tell me. I realized that I knew almost nothing about his personal life, probably because I had never asked, and I would have asked right then except that it seemed absurd to say "How's the family?" when I didn't even know if he had a family, when what I really wanted to say was "Why are you here?"

I poured him some French roast coffee and put a plate of toasted sunflower seed bread in front of him, then got feta cheese and strawberry jelly out of the refrigerator.

"Thanks," he said as he put down the paper and tried to spread the crumbly feta on his toast, then smothered it with jelly and bit in.

He didn't speak, didn't approve or disapprove of the meal, and the silence grew awkward, so I asked, "Anything interesting in the paper?"

With his mouth full he said, "Jew see where there was a man on top of the Montgomery Building yesterday said he was gone jump?"

"No, I didn't."

"It's in the paper. I know him. We used to work together over at Randolph Construction."

"What happened?"

"Police talked him down."

"Why was he up there in the first place?"

"They say he stabbed a woman."

"So, he was suicidal because he stabbed a woman?"

"It was his wife." He said it as if stabbing a wife were an offense entirely different from stabbing a non-wife woman. "Why did he stab her?"

He shrugged. Either it didn't matter or the paper didn't say. Then there was silence again, and the longer it lasted, the longer he went without explaining his presence, the greater my annoyance. I just knew he was going to finish his breakfast and leave without offering any explanation, and I couldn't have that, I would ponder it all day, so regardless of rudeness, I blurted out, "Why are you here, Landlord?"

He looked at me as if I'd hurt his feelings. "I needed a place to stay the night. I 'preciate you lettin me."

"But why?"

"I couldn't stay at home."

"Why not?"

"Me and my wife, we ain't been gettin along too good."

"You didn't stab her did you?"

"Naw," he said without any indication that he knew I was joking.

I wanted to ask him why he picked my house instead of one of his other rentals, or a friend's house, or a hotel, but I didn't want to offend him again. "I'm sorry."

"Not your fault."

"I meant I'm sorry you're having trouble. What will you do?"

"Hell if I know. I'm gone go over there in a minute, but she'll probably be at work. You got anything needs fixin while I'm here?"

The non sequitur caught me off guard, and I said, "The shower's been dripping."

"Probably needs a washer. I'll look at it."

"It's not urgent. You don't have to worry about it now."

"May's well.   Since I'm here."

In the morning the landlord was here again, his parka folded at the end of the couch. He had gotten up early and I found him painting the railing by the back steps.

"Good morning," I said through the screen door.

"It was startin to rust."

"I hadn't noticed. I guess you and your wife didn't make up."

"Naw."

"What did she say? What happened?"

"Nothin. She threw my stuff in a pile in the back yard." I imagined a mound of power tools, jeans and flannel shirts.

"So it's final?"

"For now." I wondered what that meant: final for now. I pushed open the door. "Careful, I painted the handle."

I let the door slap behind me and sat on the top step. It was a polished silver May morning, warm but not humid, and the spot where I sat enjoyed the shade of a hundred-year-old oak. If the whole summer were like this, I wouldn't miss Vermont. "Have you been to a marriage counselor or anything like that?"

"Naw."

"Do you have kids?"

"I got a boy eighteen, he'll be going off to Clemson. He'll be all right. And a girl sixteen—we're pretty close, me and her."

I was surprised—I hadn't thought of my landlord as a father, especially not a doting father with a six-teen-year-old daughter. "What's her name?"

"Cindy. After my mother, Cynthia."

"Do you still love your wife?"

He had been kneeling, painting the base of the left rail, and now he stood up, twisted his trunk both ways to stretch his back, and looked at me, squinted as if I were out of focus. "Hard to say. You forget." I thought about that for a moment and was about to ask him what, exactly, he forgot, but he asked, "You in love with that woman I've seen over here, the one with long legs and pretty hair?"

"Tess." Saying her name opened the Tess file in my brain, and there she was with all her quirks and charms. Did I love her? That was one of the BIG questions, more personal but just as ponderous as IS THERE A GOD? or HOW DO WE KNOW WE EXIST? Tess was intelligent, ambitious, and pretty in a lean and wispy way. We had been dating for eight months, and I still wanted to put my hands on her whenever she was within reach—undoubtedly, there was that. I liked going out with her to movies, restaurants, clubs—she counteracted my reclusive nature and kept me in touch with the larger community. We talked easily—she was more conservative than I, but our disagreements tended to be civil. Our main incompatibilities were that she was a fanatic exerciser and I loathed exercise for exercise's sake . . . and she was a late night-late riser, while I was an early to bed-early riser. Soon, I knew, one of us would force the issue of commitment, and we'd have to get married or break up. It occurred to me that in order to make that decision when the time came, I ought to know the answer to my landlord's question. Did I love her?

"That is a difficult question," I said. "You're dripping."

"Oh." He wiped his brush on the rim of his can, dipped it again, and resumed painting.

"Tess and I are just going out together, for now."

"Lust?"

"I wouldn't call it lust, but there is mutual physical gratification, among other pleasures."

"I like the way you talk, Philosopher. You use lots of words. Tell me somethin—you teach ethics?"

It surprised me that he knew my field well enough to ask the question. "Sometimes."

"You teach those boys and girls what's right and wrong?"

"Not exactly. I show them the complexity of the principles of deciding what's right and wrong, and we discuss difficult ethical situations, individual good versus the greater good, the categorical imperative, things like that, but they have to decide for themselves what's right and wrong."

I expected him to say, That's what's wrong with education today, but he nodded, which I took for approval. "Why?" I asked.

"You ever talk about marriage, sex, adultery?"

"Yes."

"What you tell em?"

"I don't tell them anything. We discuss the conflict

between the animal instinct to have more than one mate and the societal need to restrict and preserve monogamous marriage."

"So you don't teach em adultery's wrong?"

"No. Most of them think it is, though."

"What you think?"

"I don't think there is any absolute wrong. I'm a moral relativist."

"You mean you think right and wrong's relative?"

"Yes."

"Sounds like chicken shit to me."

"Normative ethics agrees with you. But I believe that every moral decision has to be made relative to the culture and/or situation. For example, in this country, if you eat someone you're considered the worst kind of criminal, like Jeffrey Dahmer. But if you live in a culture that practices cannibalism . . . see?"

"In this country we practice adultery, but we still think it's wrong," he said.

"As a society we think so. Individually, some of us do and some of us don't. Some believe it's wrong and do it anyway. Some don't believe it's wrong, but don't do it. There's no absolute."

"What about the law?"

"You're right, we have lots of laws that dictate morals, but in principle I disagree with them. That doesn't mean I break them." Apparently, that stumped him, or perhaps he thought he had made his case and needed to say no more. "I'm going to have some cereal—do you want some?" I stood up and dusted the seat of my bathrobe.

"Naw." I turned and just as I put my fingers on the handle, he said "Watch that handle." I pulled them away, black and sticky. "I got some turpentine in the truck." He put down his can of paint and balanced the brush on the rim, walked around the house and returned with turpentine and a rag.

"Thanks." I wiped my fingers and handed the can and rag back to him.

"I'm gone need this house," he said.

"What?"

"I need a house. I'll give you till the end of the

month to find somewheres else."

I was flabbergasted. My first thought was, He didn't say what I thought he said; then, He can't do this; and then I remembered I hadn't signed a lease or prepaid any rent. "But I've lived here a year, I've taken good care of it, I'm a good tenant."

"That's right. If I had a vacant house, I'd want you to have it, but it's one of those times I'm all full up."

"But why me, why this house?"

"It's my favorite. It was my grandmother's house. I use to spend summers here. She willed it to me when she died—that's how I got started in the business."

What could I say to that? "But what if you and your wife get back together?"

"Not likely."

"But shouldn't you wait and see?"

He had resumed painting the rail. "I tell you what, Philosopher, you a good talker, you go talk to her, see if you can fix it up. If you can, you can stay."

"But that's absurd, I don't even know your wife."

He shrugged.

I imagined searching for another house—I'd never find one as close to the school—and packing, moving—I loathed moving, the wasted time—boxing my books alone would take days—the physical exhaustion, the dust. Even more important, I had come to love this bungalow, I had fully settled into its six rooms and adapted to its claw-foot tub and other 1920s traits. And besides, I thought I might be able to help. I *was* a good talker, my mother used to tell me I should be a lawyer whenever I showed her the logical flaws of her decisions. "I'll think about it. You'd have to help me, tell me everything. And it'd be best if you came with me."

"It'd be up to her," he said.

"Ask her."

"All right."

Standing on my landlord's front porch, toting a Kentucky Fried Chicken Family Meal in two large bags, I felt idiotic, ill-prepared, and scared, but just desperate enough to keep my house to prevent me from bolting. This brick ranch house, as expected, appeared well taken care of—the yard cut and edged, flower beds weeded and mulched, eaves and windows recently painted a high gloss white—but the woman who opened the door was not what I'd expected. I'd pictured an angry, frumpy, middle-age housewife who would begrudge me a few minutes of her harried time only because I had brought over supper. Instead, I was looking at a petite red-head with a trim figure and the complexion of a thirty-year-old. She was wearing a violet sun dress with a spray of silver stars across the front—the toenails of her bare feet were violet, too. "You must be the philosopher," she said with a smile that set me at ease.

"Kevin."

"I'm Jonellen. Come in." She stepped aside and I passed. "I see you're bearing gifts—you're not Greek, are you?"

"No, Scotch-Irish."

"Then I accept." She held out her hands and I gave her the bags. "You didn't have to, you know. I would've agreed to see you anyway. Lou says you're a good talker, I believe that's how he put it. Anyway, I enjoy good conversation."

Lou, that was it—I'd forgotten my landlord's name. She led me into a combination living room-dining room, tastefully decorated in a contemporary style: a big, colorful, floral print sofa, two matching chairs with coordinated upholstery, mini blinds, light-colored rugs on hardwood floors. The rooms were rather a mess—a newspaper scattered across the sofa and a sweater wedged into the corner of it, a pair of socks curled up on the floor beside a full ash tray, a coffee cup and a glass with some previous liquid dried in the bottom—obviously she had not taken pains to straighten up for my visit. She set the bags on the dining room table and tore into them. "Mmm, barbe-cue chicken, my favorite—Lou must have told you."

"He did, I confess."

She pulled out a drumstick and took a bite. As she chewed she said, "Have a seat and I'll get us something to drink. I have beer, wine, ice tea, Coke, gin and tonic."

"There's tea here," I said and pulled a gallon jug from one of the bags. "That's what I'll have. I've come to appreciate Southern sweet tea."

She dropped the drumstick bone on the table and went through a door, to the kitchen, I assumed, but continued talking, "Where are you from, Kevin?"

"I grew up in Vermont, but did my graduate work at Vanderbilt." I set the food out on the table.

"Oh, I love Vermont in the summer. I attended a dance workshop at Bennington one summer."

"Really? Bennington is a pretty place."

She returned with paper plates, forks, and a couple of glasses.

"They gave us some plastic forks," I said.

"Good." She pushed the stainless steel ones to the side. "I hate to wash dishes. I hate all housework—that's one of our bones of contention." She paused and nodded at the table—I got it, the pun, and smiled for her. "Lou's an obsessive cleaner. He can't stand the mess I make." She poured the tea and sat down.

I was confused, and not only by her wit. I'd expected to hear a cacophony of complaints about my landlord, not a confession of sins from his wife. "Is that why you want a divorce?"

"I haven't said I want a divorce." She took another piece of chicken, a biscuit, and small helpings of baked beans and cole slaw. "Help yourself."

"You don't want a divorce?"

"I've never said the word." She looked at her chicken, not at me, as she ate.

"Then why did you throw Lou's things outside and lock him out?"

"Because I don't want him in the house unless he can act civil."

Hope surged through my blood and gave me an appetite. This dispute could be resolved, this marriage could be saved, my house could be mine. I took a big bite of a breast. "What does he have to do? What is your standard of civility?"

She was piling bones, like kindling, on the table in

front of her—she hadn't bothered to put a napkin under them.

"First of all, the man's got to talk. He would go days, literally, without speaking if no one asked him a direct question. You know him, you must have noticed."

"I admit he's not garrulous."

"Not garrulous?" She laughed. "There's a world of difference between not garrulous and mute."

"He strikes me as being shy, self-conscious, and thoughtful—surely he's always been this way, so why did you marry him if his silence annoys you?"

"Opposites attract, Philosopher, and then they spend the rest of their lives trying to change each other. Haven't you ever heard that?"

"No."

"Well it's true."

"So you've tried to change him to be more communicative, and he's tried to change you to be more neat."

"Among other things. And we've both failed."

"Then why does he get punished and you don't?"

"This isn't about punishment. It's about being unable to live with each other."

"But he loses his house and kids. You don't."

"He has a dozen houses, Philosopher. It's just your bad luck that he wants the one you're living in."

"What about the kids, then?"

"Jeff's going off to college. If it comes to that, we can work out a fair arrangement with Cindy. I don't want to deny him his precious daughter."

Ah, his *precious* daughter, a phrase loaded with mother-daughter jealousy. Was the Electra complex the cause of this crisis, and if so, what could I do about it? Before I could think of anything to say, she spoke again. "It's not what you think, Philosopher. I have a very good relationship with my daughter, but our family dynamics are complicated and, frankly, none of your business. Are you going to want more chicken?"

"No, this piece is enough. Thank you."

"You bought it. But if you don't want any more, I'll

save it for the children. They'll be home eventually."

"That's fine." She pressed the lid on the bucket and took it inside.

When she returned, carrying a pack of cigarettes and a lighter, I said, "Is there anything else, besides his not talking?"

"I have a long list, Philosopher. You want to hear it all?"

"No, just the main things, or anything you think I can help with."

She leaned back in her chair, crossed her legs though I couldn't see them, and lit a cigarette. "You really think you can help?"

"I'm committed to giving it a try."

"All right. See if you can get him to stop being mean or pouty. Those are his two moods at home, mean or pouty."

"Mean? I find that hard to believe. My landlord seems gentle and passive."

"Your landlord, is that what you call him?" She laughed again, tilting her head back, displaying a lovely neck that would never need scarves. Then she leveled a serious gaze at me. "Your landlord is passive-aggressive. He doesn't beat us, but he stomps around, slams doors, kicks things that are in his way. And when he does speak to me, it's usually to criticize. Would you want to live with someone who acted like that?"

"No, but I assume he hasn't always been that way, so I'd ask myself what caused him to become it."

"If you think you can solve our marital problems with logic, you're a bigger fool than I suspected."

A different tone, hard and cynical. So, all along she had expected me to be a fool, and she'd humored me, why? for fun? for free chicken? I was offended, and my role in this transaction grew more personal. As I considered how to respond, she blew smoke in my direction, studied me, then let me have it. "I cheated on him, Philosopher. Did he tell you that?"

"No." I wished he had. Now I felt as if I were falling off the roof of a house and my long bones were about to be crushed.

"Well, there it is."

"Is it over?"

"The affair? Yes. He was a teacher, by the way. History." She held my eyes—hers, I noticed, were blue-violet, or looked that way in the smoke and late sunlight. "And now you feel sorry for him, your poor landlord, with a cheating slut of a wife who threw him out, and you probably think, well, good riddance, but you still want that house."

"No, not at all. Yes, I want to keep the house, but mainly I'm curious. How did he find out?"

She looked out the window, into the golden pond of the sunset. "One of my girlfriends told her husband, and he told Lou."

"How did it unfold, the break-up, I mean, after he found out and yet you decided to stay together?"

She looked back at me. "It was a mess. It was awful. I cried non-stop for days."

"Why?"

"Because I didn't know what to do, to leave or stay. On the one hand, here was this handsome, sexy, articulate man who said he loved me, and on the other hand there was this silent lump who only cared about tinkering with his damn houses, but it just so happened I married him and had two children with him. I was utterly unable to make a decision, I was a basket case. When I was with Richard, I knew he was the man for me. When I was at home with my children, I knew that was where I belonged. You tell me, Philosopher, how is a human being supposed to make such a decision?"

I shook my head. "I have no idea."

"Don't your books have any answers?"

"Sure, lots of them. Obey the law, or follow the teachings of the Bible, or do the least harm, or choose what's best for the most people, or do what you wish everyone in the same circumstances would do . . . How did you decide?"

"My daughter beat up my lover." She smiled and stubbed out her cigarette. "It's funny now, but at the time it wasn't. She found him alone in his classroom after school and hit him with a tennis racket, broke

one of his fingers and gave him a mild concussion.
He didn't handle it very well, he threatened to press
charges, and I suppose that moment of weakness
settled it for me."

Just then the doorbell rang, and I said, "That's
probably Lou. I asked him to come by after you and
I had had a chance to talk awhile."

"But *I* told him not to come."

"I know, but I thought—"

"You thought you'd be in control, you thought
you'd cast a spell over me with your pretty words.
Well fuck you and Lou." She stood up and shoved her
chair with the backs of her legs so it slammed against
the wall—she was two steps from leaving.

"Wait, Jonellen." I stood, too. "That's not what I
thought. I've just heard that marriage counseling
never works unless you bring both parties to the
table. I thought maybe I could mediate, that's all."

"You're a fucking philosopher—you're not even
married—what the hell do you know about marriage?"

"I watch 'Mad About You' every week," I said.

Her scowl slowly, very slowly, turned into a one-
sided grin. "'Mad About You' has about as much to
do with my marriage as . . . as the statue of David has
to do with Lou. But it's a cute show."

"Does that mean I can let him in?"

She hesitated, shook her head, and said, "Why
not."

I turned to go to the door, but she stopped me.
"Are you finished with that?" She nodded toward the
piece of chicken that I had half eaten.

"I guess so." She reached across the table and
scooped up my paper plate and the remains of my
meal and crushed it in her hands, then stuffed it into
one of the empty paper sacks. I let Lou in.

She had resumed her seat and watched us come.
I sat where I had, across from her, and Lou sat beside
me. Neither of them spoke to the other. Jonellen lit
another cigarette and shifted her gaze back and forth
from me to Lou as if we were playing poker and she
thought both of us were going to cheat. He, lumpish,

looked back at her. I took the initiative. "Seems to
me that the two of you need to see a marriage counselor."

"He thinks that's what you are," Jonellen said.
"We all know I'm just a philosophy professor."
"And he's the landlord, and I'm the slut."
"Neither of us has called you that or thinks that,"
I said.
"Oh? Ask the landlord what he thinks."
"OK," I said, because I knew the answer, "Land-
lord, do you think your wife is a slut?"
"Naw."
She leaned toward him and shouted, "Then why
do you treat me like one? Why do you treat me like
shit?"
"I don't," he said evenly.
"You do!"
The difference in Jonellen's behavior before and
after Lou's arrival was remarkable—she seemed to
hate him. "OK," I said, "Lou, Jonellen told me that
you are mean or pouty at home, that you stomp
around and kick things, and that you never talk to her
except to criticize her. Is that right?"
"Naw."
"It is, too! You liar!" she screamed. She snatched
up one of the forks that she had originally brought
from the kitchen and threw it at him. It stuck in his
chin and hung there.
I froze, amazed. Lou slid his head back and looked
down as if he'd spilled something on his shirt; then
he reached into his back pocket, withdrew a handkerchief, pulled out the fork, and applied the handkerchief to his wound, all calm as if he had removed
forks from his chin many times before.
I looked at Jonellen, unable to guess whether she'd
apologize or throw another one. She did neither.
"I told you not to come," she said, "especially if
you're going to lie to your little philosopher friend.
Go on, admit it, admit that you're mean and pouty, or
both of you get out right now."
I was ready, I wanted to flee, but he said, "All
right."

"All right what?"

"I get mad when the house is a wreck—I cain't help it."

"Oh," she said, "all this, all the tension between us, is because the house is a mess? Give me a break."

"That's a lot of it."

"It's because I cheated on you!" she screamed, "and you can't forgive me."

My landlord didn't move, didn't blink, kept his handkerchief pressed against his chin and his gaze pressed against hers. "You loved him more'n you ever loved me. How'm I suppose to forget that?"

Suddenly there were tears in her eyes, but before they could well and fall, she dashed from the room, leaving us behind in the vacuum of her pain and anger. The house filled with the echo of silence and the shadow of the tired day, tarnished brass light.

I looked at Lou, his droopy eyes, an expression that was, well, abashed. "I'm sorry, Landlord."

"Not your fault."

"I thought I could help, but I'm afraid I've made it worse."

"It was a long shot anyway." Slowly, he pushed himself from the table with one hand while the other held the handkerchief to his chin, then he stood and headed for the front door. I looked around, feeling that I was forgetting something, then followed. As we passed through the living room, I had a view of the dark hall that led to the bedrooms, and I imagined Jonellen curled on her side in her bed, with a pillow compress wrapped around her head, as if trying to staunch the flow of words, or memory, trying to keep the re-opened wound from throbbing.

When we reached my car and his truck parked on the recently-sealed driveway, I asked a question cater-corner to the one that was on my mind, "What do we do now?"

"You got peroxide and Band-Aids?"

"Yes."

"You mind me sleeping on the couch?"

"No." I almost added "temporarily" but caught myself.

"Maybe one of my other tenants'll pull out soon."

Relieved, I said, "Or maybe she'll relent."

"Not likely," he said.

I wanted to ask another question, thought better of it, then asked it anyway. "Do you think you might be able to forgive her?"

He leaned back against the door of his truck, peeled the blood-spotted handkerchief from his chin, looked at it, then reapplied it. He glanced at the house, its glossy neatness dulled by dusk, then took in the yard and neighborhood, as if appraising that which he was about to lose. "Hard to say. It don't feel forgivable."

"The old battle of head and heart," I said.

"Whatever."

"Maybe your feelings will change with time."

"I reckon it's in your best interest to hope so."

"Well, yes, yes it is."

He fixed me with a final glance that said, I know what you're thinking, Philosopher, but that's all right. Then he climbed in his truck and, holding up his punctured chin with one hand and steering with the other into the relative darkness, he led the way to my house, to his house.

The Center of the Universe

The center of the universe barges into the guest bedroom, my office, and says "Dad," even though the door is mostly closed, even though she can see I'm trying to grade papers.

I answer without looking up. "What?"

"You said you'd help me with a story for extra credit, remember?" When I don't answer immediately, she adds, "To pull up my grade."

"Can it wait?"

"I've kinda got other plans later."

"OK, just a minute." She surveys her freckles in the mirror over the dresser while I write a comment on the paper in front of me. When I finish and turn to face her, she looks fuzzy, so I take off my glasses and hold them out to see if they're dirty or if my sight is getting even worse. Now she looks fuzzy and far away. "OK, what do you want to write about?" I put on my glasses and pull a legal pad out of my briefcase on the floor beside me.

"I don't know. You're the writer." She sits on the corner of the bed and begins to fidget, rocking, keeping time with the fast music under her teenage skin.

"I won't do this by myself, Ruthie."

"OK, OK, but I don't know how to start."

"You need a character and a problem. What's your character's name?"

"Andrea."

"Let's not write about your best friend."

"OK, Simone."

"Simone what?"

"Jenkins."

"Sounds like a French redneck. How about DesChamps?"

"I can't even spell DesChamps."

"I can." I write it down. "What's her problem?"

"She doesn't know how to spell her name." Leaning back on her elbows, she gives me her look, a tease, a slight squeeze of the eyes, mostly her left eye because her right is hidden behind a wave of red hair. She gives the look without grinning, and it always defeats me.

I sigh. "What else?"

"I don't know."

"Boys?"

"That's so boring."

"Boys are boring?" I'm about to ask why she spends every waking minute of the day talking to them on the phone if they're boring, but she says, "Boys aren't boring. Boy problems are boring."

"Oh. What then?"

She sits up again, tugs at the cuffs of her sweatshirt and presses them to the bed with her arms stiff, as if she's bracing for takeoff. "Maybe the girl could get kidnapped at the mall."

"Who would want her?"

"Daaad."

"OK, who would kidnap her and why?"

"She's rich and these guys want her money."

"Oh, I didn't know that." I jot it down.

"She's like the daughter of the guy who owns Wal-Mart, and these guys, one of them's the janitor at her school, it's a private school."

"Sam Walton died."

"Jeez. He's *like* Sam Walton. He owns Richland Mall, OK?"

"OK. But why can't we write about a normal girl with a normal problem?"

"Yeah, right. Poor Susie doesn't have a date for Homecoming. Wow. Thrills a minute."

I sit back and imagine. "Maybe Poor Susie has a

younger sister she doesn't get along with, and because they live in a tiny house, she has to share a
room with her, and she can't stand it so she runs
away to live with her best friend."

She rolls her eyes and says, "Bor-ing. What's
wrong with a kidnapping?"

I write KIDNAPPED! across my pad. "It's too
sensational. And you don't know anything about it.
How many kids do you know who've been kidnapped?"

"The same number that've run away from their
little sister."

I sigh again. This time she is grinning, or smirk-
ing, it's hard to tell. "OK, it's your story, it's your
grade."

"Maybe this isn't such a good idea." She slouches
and pulls a strand of hair in front of her left eye to
check for split ends.

"Don't give up already, Ruth."

"I didn't know it was going to be this hard.
I mean, we haven't gotten anywhere. How long does
it take you to write a story?"

"Sometimes days, sometimes months." I look at
my watch. "I don't think I've ever done one in twelve
minutes."

"Yeah, but yours are, you know, serious."

Yeah, serious. Literary. Bought for two figures,
published in journals with circulation in three figures.
But Ruth knows and cares nothing about that, so I
just say, "We have to be serious about this one too or
it won't be good."

"But I told Andrea I'd go with her to the soccer
match."

I slap the pencil down, give her my look, the
parental disapproval look, "Go then. Forget the
whole thing."

She hesitates, studying her hands as her red
fingernails drum her kneecaps. I want her to say,
You're right, Dad, let's get back to work. Instead, she
rises without saying a word and leaves.

◊

The story was Ruth's teacher's idea, but it was my idea for us to do it together. It's not a bad idea, really. In the first place, Ruth needs to bring up her grade. You can't imagine how embarrassing it is for me, a college English teacher and so-called writer, to have a D-in-English daughter. But the more important reason is that I crave to understand the teenage stranger who lives in my house. I know: My friends who have teenagers assure me it's normal—there's no more reason for me to understand Ruth than for me to understand a Mid-East terrorist. But I can't accept that, and I hoped this project would bring us closer. Writing is, after all, the most personal thing I do, except for occasional repartee with my wife.

My wife. We have our habits of peace, and she has a separate peace with Ruth. She expects Ruth to be moody, rude, egotistical, and worse during adolescence. It's a phase, she says. I went through it, too, she says. Chill out, she says. My wife can even talk like our daughter.

I'm chilling out here at my desk, which I refinished with Ruthie's help, when she was five and into helping. Back then it was me, not her, who thought she was the center of the universe. Staring at the wavy grain in the maple wood, I think of Ruthie and turn her into Poor Susie. Poor Susie lives in a trailer with her mom and sister June near Ft. Jackson, near enough so that they hear artillery practice almost every day. Boom. It drives Susie crazy. Boom. It shakes the Revlon bottles on her dresser. Boom. That and her mother's nagging and her sister's pestering drive her crazy. Drive. If she could drive, she'd take the car tonight, after her mother falls asleep, and she'd disappear. Maybe she'd go look for her daddy in North Carolina. Daddy. Four years ago he was transferred to Ft. Bragg and simply refused to take them along. She doesn't know if she loves him or hates him. Maybe she'd go to Atlanta, lie about her age, get a job.

I'm in Poor Susie's head, picking up her thoughts, examining them, putting them back, when my wife comes home from work, still wearing her white lab coat. "Hey," she says as she passes my door on the way to our bedroom to change. "Where's Ruthie? I thought y'all were going to work on a story."

"She and Andrea had a prior engagement to ogle the boys at the soccer match."

"Hmmm," is my wife's response, as if Ruth probably made the right choice.

Maybe her mother spoke to her, or maybe she is more embarrassed by her grade than I think, but the next night Ruth returns. She doesn't apologize or grovel. She just nudges the door and appears, one shoulder leaning against the doorjamb. "Dad, will you help me with the story some more?"

I put down my copy of *Julius Caesar* and think about giving in. "I guess I can spare another twelve minutes," I say to let her know that if she expects my help, I expect her commitment. She plops down and leans against the headboard of the bed, arms folded over the flat chest that is one of her constant preoccupations, along with her thin lips, ski-jump nose, Biblical name, and so much more. Today she has crimped a two-inch star into her wave of hair, and I remember hearing her mention the instrument of such desecration to her mother, but I don't remember hearing them say they might actually buy it. I push away my book and pull out the legal pad on which I jotted our notes. "OK. I thought up some ideas for Poor Susie—do you want to hear them, or do you want to stick with Simone The Kidnapee?"

"Simone."

I'm disappointed, but it's her story. "OK. You said her dad owns Richland Mall. What does her mother do?"

"Nothing. They're rich."

"What about in her free time—does she play tennis at the country club or volunteer for Meals on Wheels?"

"She plays tennis."

"Mall-magnate Dad, is he ever home, and what's his relationship with his daughter?"

"I don't know. How am I supposed to know all

this stuff? What does it matter, anyway?"

"This stuff is the background that will make your character believable. But we can get right to her if you think parents aren't important." Pause to let that sink in. "OK, what does Simone want?"

Ruth gives her look and says, "She wants to get away from the kidnappers."

"I mean besides that, before she gets kidnapped."

"She wants to have fun."

"What does she think is fun?"

"Going to the mall with her friends."

"That's her goal in life, to go to the mall with her friends?"

"Daaad."

"That's what you said."

She sulks or thinks. Then, without looking up she says, "She wants to be happy."

The way she says it, simply and sincerely, without the usual sneer, trips my heart. She wants to be happy. I see Simone hiding behind a wave of red hair. "But why, honey?" The term slips out of the past—I used to call her honey all the time but don't anymore. "Why is Simone unhappy?" I try to catch her gaze, but she keeps her head down as she tugs at a rhinestone on her T-shirt.

"She doesn't know."

"Is she ugly?" I ask.

"No."

"Unpopular?"

"No."

"Do *you* know why she's unhappy?"

"How should I know when she doesn't know?"

"Exactly," I say. Ruth doesn't hear or else ignores me. I press on. "Does she have a boyfriend?"

"What about the kidnapping, Dad?"

"OK, do the kidnappers have boyfriends?"

"Dad, you're such a dork."

"Is that good or bad?"

"I can't handle this, Dad." She gets up and walks to the door. "I've got to study math."

"Stay, Ruthie. I won't joke around anymore."

"I've got a test tomorrow, or do you want me to

make a D in that, too?" She knows I'll have no smart answer to this.

"Go then," I say, and she does.

I follow Ruthie to the mall on Friday night because I want to see what happiness she thinks she finds there.

She and her friends spend most of their time in Flickers, the arcade. I can't go in because they'd see me, but I assume, I hope, they're playing video games. Finally, as I watch, fifty yards away, from a bench partially hidden behind a planter of scheffelera, they emerge, one girl and boy holding hands, another boy chasing and tagging Ruthie. She seems to be complaining, but playfully, and when he isn't expecting it, she tags him back hard on the shoulder.

Ruthie's boy takes a pack of cigarettes out of his shirt pocket and offers them around—the other guy and girl accept, but Ruthie, I'm relieved, does not. The other couple drifts to the benches in the center of the aisle, as if smoking is hard work and they need a rest. Ruthie and the boy she tagged hover near the entrance to the arcade. She leans back against the wall—she's taller than him but leaning back brings her down a few inches. As he moves in close to her, her arms encircle his waist. They kiss, seriously if clumsily, mashing their bodies, oblivious to the turning heads of shoppers.

I get up and take a step toward them so I can kill the boy.

But I stop, knowing that to break them up, even to show myself, would be disastrous for my relationship with my daughter. I sit back down. We can both live with her thinking I'm a dork—I probably am one—but she'd never forgive my being a spy or policeman. Policeman. That's how I feel, here to make sure there's no trouble. Trouble. This scene looks like trouble, feels like trouble, but why?—because she's too young—is fourteen too young to kiss?—no, but it will lead to sex—am I sure?—yes, no, not sure but

worried. Worried. She's my little girl and if that boy .
. . I watch his hands, one of which is down at his side,
holding his cigarette—thank God he smokes—but the
other is on the side I can't see. Paralyzed, I watch.

Although I lose all sense of time, I'm pretty sure
the kiss does not last long before Ruthie pushes the
boy away. Silently I cheer her on to kick him and
gouge his eyes out, but she merely catches his jacket
sleeve and drags him across the aisle to the music
store.

I breathe again and wipe my foggy glasses. I feel
tired as if I've been chasing someone for miles.
Thrills a minute. Happiness. Is this what she wants:
clumsy kisses from a short boy with cigarette breath?

Go then, I say to her in my head, You can handle
this trouble, and you'll outgrow it soon enough.

Feeling useless, I turn to leave. As I glance back
one last time to check on my daughter and her
boyfriend's hands, I see a door to a storage room and
think, that's where it would happen, that's where
Simone would be kidnapped. On the way home, I
plot the story of how Simone's father arranges a
kidnapping to shock his daughter into loving her life
again. I wonder if Ruthie will be happy with it.

On George Singleton

by Fred Chappell

I HAVE A LONG AND UNHEALTHY ACQUAIN-
TANCE WITH BARS, JOINTS, AND DIVES AND WITH
THE FOLKWAYS THERETO, AND I HAVE NEVER HEARD OF
a security man called the "pre-bouncer." According to
the narrator of George Singleton's story, "Outlaw
Head and Tail," his duties are simple but important.
"If some guy came into the Treehouse and looked like
he meant trouble, I was to go up to him and start a
little conversation, let him know this wasn't the kind
of place to throw a punch without inelegant and
indubitable consequences."

In fact, I don't think there is such a thing as a pre-
bouncer, nor any drinking establishment called the
Treehouse, all fixtured with tree trunks like a room of

a forest. But the germane question is, in both cases, "Shouldn't
there be?" I'd like to sample the
wares of the Treehouse and I'd
feel, if not safer, then at least
warmly gratified if a pre-bouncer
was on duty.

It is one of Mr. Singleton's
salient gifts to make us so well
disposed toward his fictions that
we first wish such situations did
exist and then at least persuade
ourselves that they might—they
can—they *do*. And since they do,
the personalities engaged with
them, and the incidents that take
place inside them, are their
inevitable accouterments. These
events work out in the only ways

they possibly can; the people in these stories are the ones we must unavoidably meet in the Treehouse, in the hapless flooded street full of wrecked mannequins, in Christ Almighty, North Carolina.

There doubtless exists some killjoy tribe of critics who, hearing the outlines of these stories without having actually read them, would describe them as farfetched and unbelievable. But if they did take the trouble to peruse Mr. Singleton's sentences, they would sing a different cantata, believe you me. Anyone who nibbles a bit of the frosting on one of these stories is going to devour the whole flavorsome cake. There is an ineluctable force of persuasion that flows from the sentence, "My father promised a quarter for every head I recovered," all the way to the end, to the narrator's determination never to visit a wax museum ever again.

In wishing that Mr. Singleton's ingenious and humane situations did exist, we are also pulling for his stories to succeed. He has trapped us into a happy collusion in the working out of his tales. A dangerous ploy, this, for what we read with affection we also read with the closest scrutiny, and if there is a misstep in the course of the circumstances, a sentence or phrase that doesn't fit comfortably the voice of its speaker, or any note struck out of key, we will be immediately and regretfully aware. The three stories here are flawless, but surely Mr. Singleton must have written some stories that don't succeed. I imagine myself reading one of these, noting a faulty passage, and saying with heartfelt ruse, "Too bad, really . . ." With other writers I might say, "I just *knew* he wasn't going to bring it off."

I can think of many writers whose work I admire immensely but with whose stories I engage without entirely letting down my guard. Throughout the pages of *Dubliners* and *In Our Time*, I keep one eye on the story and the other on the authors, determined not to allow them to put anything over on me. But I want Mr. Singleton to succeed with whatever strategy it takes. "Deceive me, sir," I plead. "Pull the wool over my gimlet eyes, practice any sly confidence trick you know because I so dearly want this story to be perfect that I'll be nigh heartbroken if it isn't."

My apprehensions are probably pointless. Probably the skew talent it requires to imagine these stories already entails the virtuoso skills needed to make them triumphs. When I think of the temptation to ruin here—cuteness, self-indulgent digression, flippancy—and wonder how the author has avoided them, I am probably only indulging in autobiographical fantasies. Those are the dangers I would have to circumvent. They probably never presented themselves to Mr. Singleton in the first place. These are the stories he was born to write. He is unique in the same way they are unique, and every atom belonging to them belongs as good to him. It is this uniqueness that gives his voice its ring—no, its tingle—of authority. Mr. Singleton is able to aver, along with the narrator of his deftest tale, that "unlike most people, I'm now allowed to stomp on this earth."

—Fred Chappell is the author of six novels, thirteen volumes of poetry and two books of short stories. He is writer-in-residence at the University of North Carolina-Greensboro.

Outlaw Head and Tail

Normally I couldn't have made the tape that Saturday. Right away, right there during the job interview a few weeks before, my soon-to-be boss had said, "Ricky, is there anything about this job that you have a problem with?"

I didn't say, "I can't work for a man who ends sentences with prepositions." I couldn't. It was a job bouncing, or at least talking. I was going to be some-thing called a "pre-bouncer." If some guy came into the Treehouse and looked like he meant trouble, I was to go up to him and start a little conversation, let him know this wasn't the kind of place to throw a punch without inelegant and indubitable consequences.

I have a way with words. I'm synonymous with rapport.

I said to Frank, "Well, I'd rather not work Saturday days, 'cause my wife has to go to temple and I have to drive her over there. I don't go to temple. Hell, I don't even go to church," I said. I said, "I don't mind working Sundays, but I'd really like it if you could get someone to work afternoons on Saturday for me. Night?—Saturday night—I'll be here. The only thing I ask of you is that I don't work Saturday afternoons, say, until six o'clock."

Frank said, "You know, you talked me into it. Man, what a way with words! It's a deal. You're a godsend, Ricky. I lucked out getting you as a pre-bouncer."

Frank had opened the Treehouse a year earlier but

didn't hire a bouncer or pre-bouncer right away. About the same time his insurance agent told him his payments would soon double, though, he hired me and a guy named Sparky Voyles to keep things down. During his first year Frank put in claims for a whole new set of glasses, from shot and snifter to the special two-foot beer glasses he ordered, plus twelve tables, sixteen chairs, another tree stump to replace the one that caught on fire and caused smoke damage to the ceiling, and forty-two stitches to his own head one night after a fearful brawl erupted over whether Chevys or Fords would dominate the circuit in the upcoming season.

Frank bought the Treehouse because of insurance, ironically. He'd worked in the pulpwood trade and a load of logs slipped off a truck he stood behind, came rolling right off like a giant wave, clipped him behind the knees so hard they said he could run as fast backwards as forwards there for a few days.

Of course, he couldn't run at all, and had to get fake knees installed. His lawyer also got him another quarter-million dollars or so due to a lifetime worth of pain and subsequent nightmares. Frank took most of that money and made the Treehouse, a regular small warehouse he furnished with tree trunks from floor to ceiling so if you blindfolded someone and took him inside the bar, then took off the mask and showed him around, he'd have the feeling that the whole building was up above the ground, built into the forest.

So during the first year there were fights and insurance claims, but the second year started right off with me and Sparky there to quiet things down. Frank didn't want us to be too heavy-handed, though. He didn't want the bar to end up so quiet it looked like a flock of mute birds built their nests in the Treehouse. He only asked for stability.

Sparky went the same route as Frank—he worked at the railroad before becoming a bouncer, getting paid under the table because he took in disability checks from when his thumbs got cut off between two boxcars that clanged together and weren't supposed to, and he thought he could prevent it from happening. He couldn't. Sparky had been a brakeman originally, out of Lexington.

Anyway, I worked hard pre-bouncing, and kept up with what I had to know, which was mainly words. This is how I get back to the tape and that Saturday. What I'm saying is, because I'm so conscientious about my job, it could've killed my marriage.

On the previous Thursday, Jessie went in to her doctor's office to have him finally go ahead and do that sonogram thing. She couldn't wait to know what our first baby was going to be, building her argument around the fact that we didn't make all that much money and if it was a boy we needed to pinch even harder and save up for his circumcision.

Jessie works as a freelance interior decorator. She got her degree in art history and felt like it gave her the right.

I took Jessie down to the doctor's office, but she couldn't get an appointment before four o'clock in the afternoon. I got clearance from Frank to get off work on Thursday, but that meant I had to come in Saturday morning at eleven 'cause the guy who normally worked Saturdays needed to go to a wedding anyway. It ended up a simple and clean swap. There didn't seem to be that much of a problem.

So I took my wife to the doctor and she did what she had to do, but the doctor still couldn't even take a stab at it, for the baby kept turned around the whole time. I was hoping it'd be a girl. I never have seen myself as being the father of a shy son.

Two days later I drove Jessie to synagogue. I drove back home in time to throw in a tape and set the VCR so I wouldn't miss "Bonanza," which showed in syndication every Saturday on one of the cable channels. I set the station and time to record, then left for the bar.

I watch "Bonanza" every week. That's where I get my ways. That's where I get my ability to talk people out of starting fights. One time this burly truck driver-type came in and seemed upset that a white guy came into the Treehouse with an African-American woman. There'd been a similar episode on "Bonanza" one time when Hoss piped up to a stranger, "Well, would you rather be blind and not have to see the ways of the world?" He said it to a redneck, of course. Words of wisdom, I thought right there and then. I'd thought "words of wisdom" on more than one occasion while watching Ben Cartwright bring up his boys the best he could. I remembered watching "Bonanza" when I was a boy, too, and how I admired the way Little Joe and Hoss and even Adam handled themselves in town. My father, though, used to throw beer cans at the television set and say, "What them boys need to use a little more often is their trigger fingers, not their tongues."

It's that kind of thinking that makes it almost amazing that I grew into being a pre-bouncer. If I'd taken my father seriously back in the sixties, I'd've ended up being something more secluded and self-centered, something like a bookkeeper, or a jockey.

I said to the burly guy, "Hey, there's two things that can happen here: either you can learn to understand that love is blind, or I can get Sparky to come over here with his eight remaining fingers and blind you himself, so you don't have to live with seeing interracial dating in your midst. Comprende, amigo?"

I pointed at Sparky. Without his thumbs it looks like he could use his fists as skewers. The truck driver looked over at Sparky, back to me, then to the white guy and black girl. He said, "Well, okay then," just like that. I stood my ground and tried not to shake. The little voice in my head kept thanking the Cartwrights over and over.

So I put the tape in the VCR, and I set the station and time, and drove off to the Treehouse. The bar doesn't open until noon, but I got there at eleven in order to help Frank clean up from the night before and to set out our specials in the plastic stand-up signs for each table. Frank said, "How goes it, Ricky?"

I said, "Okay, I guess. You?"

Frank said, "Uh-huh. Fine." He said, "You know,

we didn't really get to talk last night. I mean, I heard you say that you still didn't know if you'd have a little boy or a girl, but what else did the doctor say?"

I wiped off a table. Friday night had been pretty slow at the Treehouse. Down the road there'd been a yearly festival with a battle of the bands and a tractor pull. I said, "He didn't say much. He asked if she'd been taking care of herself, whether she'd quit drinking and smoking. She said she had, which is true and goddamn, it ain't fun around the house, by the way. And then he said he thought her delivery date might need to be changed about a week early. Not much else went on. He dabbed some goo on her big stomach and we saw this little crooked Vienna sausage-looking thing on the television screen. Then he gave us the tape."

Well, no, I said, "The *tape!* "

I didn't say good-bye to Frank. I didn't tell him I'd be right back. I just left the Treehouse, got in my car, and drove fifteen minutes back to my house.

It was too late. Right over the image of my as-yet-sexless child, the floating little thumb-sucking thing inside Jessie's body, Hoss now talked to little Joe about how skittish the horses seemed to be all of a sudden.

Sparky said, "Well, it could be worse, Ricky. At least she still has the baby. One time when I was working Amtrak, this woman came screaming out of the bathroom saying she'd miscarried in the toilet. We were flying down the track about sixty miles an hour, you know. I had my break and was eating an egg salad sandwich in the dining car. I remember all this 'cause I had a mouthful of egg in my mouth when this woman made the announcement."

I nodded my head and shoulders quickly, trying to get Sparky to finish the story. I needed to make some phone calls, or talk to some of the customers.

Sparky said, "She came running out of that bathroom saying the thing came out of her, she thought, but she wasn't sure. On a train, you know, it goes straight down to the track, and at sixty miles an hour you don't have time to exactly check what came out in the bowl underneath you. One time I had a kidney stone and I was supposed to be pissing into a strainer, but I kept forgetting. So I have a stone in between the tracks somewhere from Lexington to Danville."

I nodded hard, waved my right hand like a paddlewheel for Sparky to finish up. A group of four women came into the Treehouse, all of them in their mid-thirties. I needed to find a way to talk to them.

"This woman on the train—her name ended up being Brenda—had a nervous breakdown right there and then. She fainted. Two men who were afraid of airplanes and traveled on business trips up to New York all the time got up and grabbed her, checked her heartbeat and breathing, and put a pillow behind her head. I said, 'Damn, you don't see this everyday on an Amtrak train, do you?' Well, as it ended up, we took her off the train at the next stop and sent her to the local hospital. That would be Gaffney—we were doing the run down to New Orleans—and then on our way back up she waited there at the station for me. She got on board and said, 'I want you to tell me exactly where we were when I miscarried. I want you to take me to the spot so I can give my baby a proper burial.' I told her that by this time—a couple days had gone by—surely her miscarriage was gone. But she got on board the train and took it up to Charlotte, and then we got out and started walking back south on the tracks. My boss said I had to do it, and that I'd probably get a raise for the whole thing."

Two more women walked into the bar. I waved my arm faster for Sparky to get to the moral of the story.

"We found about twenty turtle shells," said Sparky. "You wouldn't believe how many turtles get stuck in between the tracks, especially snapping turtles when you're near a lake or in the swamps. We found turtle shells, and that was it. I wasn't even sure what I was supposed to be looking for. And if I did run across anything that looked like a baby, I didn't want to see it, or point it out to Brenda. So as it ended up, after I finally convinced her that we'd gone past the spot where she miscarried, she walked over into the woods and got some sticks. She borrowed my shoelaces and fashioned a small wooden cross, stuck it a few feet from the track, and said she felt better. And an hour later this gandy dancer came from the station to pick us up to get us back to the station. I wonder whatever happened to old Brenda?" Sparky asked, like I'd know.

He walked off with his hands in his pockets, straight down like trowels were attached to the ends of his arms. I lost all pride and any bashfulness whatsoever and started asking women if they had any of their sonogram videotapes around their houses. I offered a hundred dollars to buy one of them.

Teresa Smiley said she'd be right back. Teresa Smiley said she kept hers on her bookshelf stuck between a 12-Step program book and a Steven King novel. Since her husband had gotten custody of their little boy, she got depressed thinking about it, but said, "A hundred dollars! Hell, I won't sell for less than *three* hundred."

It was one of those occasions when I didn't have time to check out the going rate for sonograms on the black market. So I said, "One-fifty." I said, "Lookit, unless you had your sonogram on Thursday, there's going to be a different date down there on the screen. I mean, I'm going to have to go to great lengths of finding out a way to forge the video."

Teresa Smiley stared hard at me, then sat back down at her table, a table filled with women who worked third shift at the mill. Teresa said, "The memory of a child is worth more than a hundred and fifty dollars, Ricky. And your wife won't even notice the wrong date down there. We women are interested in the baby, not the time of day. I'm insulted, and you should be ashamed."

"A minute ago," I said, "you were saying how you got depressed even knowing the tape was around. Come on, Teresa, you don't know how much I need this tape." I told her my story, but didn't explain about "Bonanza" over the image of my baby. I told her it was professional wrestling, so she could understand why I might be a little distraught about having to work on Saturday in the first place.

Teresa said, "Two-fifty," I said, "Two," and she left to get the tape. I didn't even ask her if her child, too, was turned away from the camera, and if it wasn't turned away, was it real obvious as to the sex of the child. When I saw ours, I wasn't even sure where was the head and where was the tail. To me, Jessie's sonogram looked like a picture of an ulcer or something on her stomach wall. I couldn't make out a meaning whatsoever. I didn't have that art background that Jessie could boast about.

Sparky came over to me a few minutes after Teresa left and said, "You might have some trouble coming at you, but I'll be there for you."

I said, "What do you mean?" The worst thing that could happen, I thought, was for Jessie's meeting to be canceled and her coming to the Treehouse to spend the day.

Sparky said, "What I'm trying to tell you is, don't turn around immediately, but there's a guy down at the end of the bar staring a hole through you. It's Teresa's ex."

I didn't turn at all. I could feel the guy staring straight into my brain. The Treehouse had its regulars who came in every day—house painters, self-employed body shop men, the disabled, people who only really worked on Wednesday mornings over at the flea market—but there were people who came in haphazardly, maybe once a month to sit by themselves and get over whatever it was that stuck in their craw. I never had to pre-bounce any of those people. First, it wouldn't matter—if they wanted to fight they'd fight no matter what I had to say. Second, most of them were so consumed with whatever bothered them, they didn't have the energy to actually get off the barstool and start a fight, though they'd probably like to see one.

I said to Sparky, "The one who got custody? Are you talking about Teresa's husband who ended up with the kid?"

He said, "That's the one. Name's Ted, but everyone calls him Slam. He won the state wrist wrestling
championship four years in a row, and the southeast
tournament twice."

I said, "Goddamn it." I thought, if only I'd taken
the time to look at the videotape before I threw it in
to tape "Bonanza." I thought, if only the baby had
turned around so we'd know the sex of it. I thought,
if only Jessie hadn't gotten the appointment on Thursday, and almost caught myself thinking, if only I'd put
on a rubber that night.

Sparky said, "I arm wrestled him one time, but it's
hard for me to get a grip, what without a thumb. Hell,
it was hard for him, too. I kept sliding right through
his hand."

"Shutup Sparky," I said, and walked straight over
to Slam. I said, "Your ex-wife's about to save my life,
man. I screwed up and taped over my child-to-be's
videotape inside the womb, and Teresa's going to get
y'all's so I can make a tape of it." I said, "My name's
Ricky."

Slam said, "Wife."

I said, "Excuse me?" He didn't look my way. He
seemed to keep staring at where I stood talking to
Sparky.

"Not ex-wife. Wife. Just like a piece of paper can't
make a marriage, a piece of paper can't end one
neither," said Slam.

I said, "Are you Catholic?"

This is no lie. Slam said, "I'm an American and
it's the American way of being."

I said, "Oh. Well, then your *wife* is about to save
my skin."

Tape the *tape*, I thought. I thought, you should've
asked her to tape the tape. I mean, there wasn't a
reason for me to pay so much to more or less wipe
hers. I tried to think of a way of getting to her before
she even got inside the Treehouse so we could at least
re-negotiate.

Slam said, "What?" He held his beer in a way I'd
not seen before, a half-inch from his face and a quar-

ter-inch to the right. At first I thought he used the can
as a mirror to check out someone who walked up
behind him. Being a pre-bouncer, I notice things like
that.

I said, "Your wife's saving my ass."

There's this look that only certain people can give.
There's this look some people can give that's somewhere between smoke in their eyes and hand gre-
nades in their pockets. Slam had that look. I turned
my head towards Sparky but he'd already started
punching a guy named Hull who came in drunk and
wanted a piece of another guy named Dayton for not
painting his house evenly earlier in the summer.

Slam said, "Well, I guess that's better than *hump-
ing* your ass, Bo."

He said, "Glad to hear it," grabbed his beer and
left the bar, either unaware of the law, or unconcerned
about the police that regularly parked across the
street.

Sparky came over and said, "You got a way with
words, Ricky. Whatever it is you said, you did it,
man."

I sat down on the bar stool next to Slam's and
concentrated so as not to actually pee in my pants
like in the cartoons.

As soon as Jessie had taken that one-minute-and-
you-know-if-you've-really-missed-your-period test in
the bathroom, she pulled a Walkman out of the bedroom closet, put in new batteries, and slipped a tape
of Mahler's Fourth Symphony in the cassette holder.
She pulled the earpieces of the headset as far apart as
possible, strapped them around her sides, and put the
volume on full blast. Jessie said, "We're going to have
a baby, Ricky."

I'd just been watching her from the other side of
the room. I didn't even know about the bathroom
test. I sat there on the side of the room reading my
thesaurus. "A baby?" I said. "Are you sure?"

She said, "I have this theory. I believe that if you
play music inside the womb, the fetus absorbs it and

when the baby comes out, instead of crying and screaming, it'll make noises similar to an orchestra."

I said, "What?"

She said, "The reason why a baby always wails is because it absorbs the noises of the outside world for nine months. In the city it hears horns honking, people screaming, the conglomeration of people's conversations all going into one big drone, dogs barking, cats crying out in the night, the hiss of a teapot . . . " She had a list of every possible noise, it seemed. She finally finished her dictum with, "So if I keep playing classical music, when the baby's in pain or wants a bottle, we'll be serenaded with French horns and oboes, the violin. Bassoons!" She said, "Bassoons! And piccolos and flutes and cellos."

Hell, to me it didn't sound like all that bad a theory. I mean, it's logically possible. I said, "Why don't you order some of those books on tape, and then at night the baby can tell *us* stories."

Jessie put another Walkman on her own ears and left the room. She kind of left the room a lot during her pregnancy, for that matter, I'm not sure why, I've always tried to be sensitive to her needs.

Ted, or Slam, whatever, kept standing outside the Treehouse. He waited for his ex-wife Teresa, I knew. Just about the time I started to go outside to tell him I wouldn't make a tape of his pre-born child, she tapped me on the shoulder. Like every intelligent woman with a lunatic ex-husband in her life, she sensed danger. She parked the Buick a few blocks away and took the back entrance. I said, "Ted's here."

She looked around. She said, "Ted was in here earlier but I don't see him now."

I said, "Out front."

"Oh. Well. Good," she said. "That'll be two hundred dollars up front, no check."

I only had a check. I said, "Hey look, I got this better idea. Why don't we find another VCR, and do a tape-to-tape so you don't have to lose yours totally. I mean, some day you might want it back." I kind of saw a big confrontation ahead, like when birth mothers arrange for adoptive parents, then change their minds in the delivery room.

Teresa said, "I won't change my mind, believe you me. I've had it. I want a new life, Bubba. As a matter of fact, I've already contacted the paper to advertise a yard sale for next weekend. I'm getting rid of my old high school yearbooks, too."

I said, "Well, okay." It was nearly three o'clock and I couldn't take the chance of Jessie getting a ride home from the synagogue with one of her friends, slipping in her tape, and fainting when she came to believe that her baby suddenly gained a clear and distinct shape and form which looked like Hoss. I said, "Hold on a second."

I bought Teresa a drink on my monthly tab and walked over to where Sparky stood in the corner of the bar, scanning the slim crowd. "Sparky," I said, "look, do you have one of those teller cards by any chance? I lost mine in the machine—not 'cause I didn't have any money—because the back strip got dirty or something and it's Saturday and the bank's closed and I need two hundred bucks right now to buy off the tape. I can give you a check today, or if you wait until Monday morning I can go over to the bank and get cash for you."

Sparky said, "I hope you remember this when you go and name your child."

I said, "I can't name my kid *Sparky*."

Sparky said, "I wouldn't expect you to." He reached into the wallet he kept chained to his belt loop and pulled out two hundred one dollar bills. He said, "My given name's Earl. Earl for a boy, Earline for a girl."

I don't know why I said okay, but I did. I figured if I could get Sparky drunk later on in the evening maybe he'd forget the promise.

"Here you go," I said to Teresa. She handed me the tape. She handed me her own personal sonogram videotape of the only child she'd ever had and said, "I hope I picked up the right one. Slam and me did some amateur strip stuff one night, but we never sent it off to any of those programs on cable."

I asked Sparky to cover for me, told him to use the

word "discretionary" or "castigatory" should a fight
seem imminent, and took the back door out, too.

There is a Supreme Being. Someone powerful
exists, or at least existed for me that afternoon. I
pulled out my tape filled with "Bonanza," plus a half
hour special on the NASCAR season at the halfway
point, and pushed Teresa's baby's video in my machine. It didn't need rewinding. I wondered if she'd
ever really watched it.

It wasn't her strip show. Right there on the
screen, in brilliant shades of gray, was a form. I
couldn't make out eyes or genitals. There was no way
possible Jessie could see the difference between her
womb and that of a woman who grew up and lived in
a mobile home.

I felt good about living in America.

The Supreme Being stayed on my side, 'cause
while the tape still played, in walked Jessie, home
from what ended up being a committee meeting of a
group called Sisters of Bashemath, Ishmael's Daughter. She said, "I thought you had to work."

I moved closer to the television screen, down on
the carpet, and held my forearm parallel to the date
and time logo down at the bottom. I said, "I went
and got things going, but I started feeling a little
nauseated."

Jessie came up to me, all smiles, and put her hand
on the back of my neck. She said, "That's so sweet.
You have sympathy pains."

I knelt on the floor in front of the TV screen.
I could hear Mahler's First Symphony playing out of
the cassette attached to Jessie's stretched sash. I
said, "Well, yeah, I had some pains all right but I'm
feeling much better now."

Jessie asked me to rewind the sonogram. I
clenched my teeth, rewound it, prayed to all the
superior beings ever invented for her not to notice
the difference.

And she didn't. While I watched Teresa's child
float around in her belly, Jessie lowered the volume

on her Walkman and pushed her chin in towards her stomach. She said, "We're watching you right now, honey."

I didn't say anything about any kind of name recognition, like, "We're looking at you Earl or Earline."

I sat and watched. And I thought to myself, certainly I want my own child to grow up and be happy and famous and healthy and intelligent. I thought, I want to be able to spend time with my kid, go to games, teach him or her how to communicate, take long trips across the country to see how different people live.

And deep down, oddly, I kind of wanted the kid I watched on the television screen to end up a bandit and a folk hero. I wanted that obscure head and tail I saw on the screen to grow up and be an outlaw of sorts, a fugitive. At that very moment I knew that I'd always keep up with Ted and Teresa's boy, and help him out whenever it seemed possible. I'd tell him to keep moving, always, in order to stay content, to talk to strangers no matter how scary it may seem.

How I Became a City Planner, with a Minor in History

My father promised a quarter for every head I recovered. He'd not owned the wig shop half a year before a series of tornadoes came through town and happened to somehow suck out his storefront picture window. I've never understood physics, but I bet there's some kind of action/reaction kind of dictum which proved itself when every styrofoam wig holder blew out onto the sidewalk, and spun down the street blocks away. I got a dollar apiece for each wig or fall, for even though they were probably useless my father believed he might have to prove his losses to some mid-level insurance agent from the home office down in Jacksonville.

My father had bought the wig shop for two reasons: He needed an investment, and he believed that women in my hometown would be losing their hair more so because of increased toxic dumping down at the underground Savannah River nuclear plant waste mall. This was 1972. I was fourteen years old with just enough hormones, pubic wisps, and sense of self to not want to walk around with a found shopping buggy filled with fake heads and Chinese women's cut hair. My friends rode around with their parents looking at the aftermath and blew their horns for me to either get out of the middle of Montague Avenue or quit looting.

My father said, "Say, if you happen to find anything else that could be mistook for hair or head,
bring it along, too. Goddamn, I might be able to get
enough insurance money to open up a roofing company. Asbestos will come into play before long, believe you me."

I'd brought the first load back, which got me six
dollars and fifty cents—big money back then for one
hour's work. There was a rain that came with—and
then followed—the tornadoes, though, and I wanted
better shoes. I came back to my father to ask him if
he minded driving over to a shoe store a couple miles
down the road to see if any of their galoshes blew out
their window. I said, "There's a bunch of insulation
blown down that way. If you talk some man into
believing you sell pink wigs you might make a killing.
I'll help you tease fiberglass for a couple dollars a
wig."

I'm not lying. That's how I talked, even at the age
of fourteen. It ran in the family. My father called his
wig store Follicle Follies.

He held a mop and said, "We ain't got time for
shoes. You get what you got to get, and I'll get what
I'm going to get." My father held his mop still. He
wore my mother's yellow slicker unbuttoned, and the
sleeves came down to just past his elbows. "Say, if
you notice any gutters blown off on your walk, make
a mental note where they are. I've been thinking
about fixing up the house back home."

I took a right off Montague Avenue, walked down
Waller Street, and found a liquor store that no longer
had a roof. Just like in those documentaries,
though—when mobile homes fly two miles down the
road, land straight up, and later on people find out
that the goldfish still lives in its water-filled globe,
that the family portrait photograph with the people
standing in front of a fake waterfall is still nailed to
the wall—nothing had moved inside the liquor store.
Whoever owned the joint had a pyramid display of
bourbon bottles six feet tall, and it still stood proudly,
like some kind of amber beacon.

At least it stood until I put my shopping cart on

top of the dumpster outside that had flipped over, then crawled on it to the top of the wall where the soffit and fascia once met, and leaped down, and pulled twelve bottles from the middle of the display until the entire thing toppled over, then unlocked and went right out the front door. Again, I had never understood physics.

I knew local geography, though, and stashed most of my goods in an ancient and historic spring house behind the Lutheran church where only something like four people outside the preacher met once a week.

Let me say now that I did have a capacity to notice the effort of Nature, questioned God, wondered what the poor dry cleaning guy would think once he saw how many times he'd get yelled at later, and saw smiles on the faces of old black men collecting lost awnings to re-sell at Harvley's junkyard. I pushed my squeaky flagellate-wheeled buggy around, looking for what my father did or didn't once own, and never thought to look towards any horizon should danger reappear.

When I got back to Follicle Follies with another ten heads and I don't know how many bouffants, I said to my father, "These were on the streets, right up against the curb. I can't believe they didn't break. There's broken glass all over the place, but I found these sitting upright next to a storm drain."

My father took the wigs and styrofoam heads first and lined them up in the rows he'd decided, in order of cost, et cetera. He said, "Hotdamn, two quarts of Old Crow," and promised me a big tip, and said I had some of his good Mayhew blood in me, and seemed to forget at the moment that a tornado ruined his wig shop.

He didn't call me by my given name, though, even after a disaster, not that I think that's something to point out if I should ever need and get some kind of psychological evaluation.

I don't believe much in predestination in regards

to individuals, as opposed to that free will argument, so it's difficult to explain how I feel that the place where I grew up had some kind of curse imposed on it that affected the entire citizenry. The main employer was a series of cotton mills from back into the nineteenth century, and maybe all the czars who built mill villages in the name of utopia somehow invited nothing but disaster, both natural and unnatural, which bore down low on the town in a crippling way not unlike trace amounts of strychnine sped through everybody's bloodstream. In the local newspaper obituaries there was only an age, list of remaining relatives, and the time of the funeral service, seeing as everyone knew where the dead person spent his years toiling.

Listen, after I sucked down about a half-pint of Old Crow it didn't seem to matter much that I walked through town wet-footed as a short snapping turtle. I pushed my cart all over, through two mill villages, past the two dozen stores that lined Main Street, down two alleys where old black men hung out on weekends, and through a cemetery. I said hello to little blind Mickey—maybe the smartest man in town—and he said, "I've never seen anything like it, Warren Jr. Tornadoes. Damn."

Little blind Mickey wasn't really blind. He wore sunglasses all the time, just so he could walk his dog everywhere and take it inside restaurants, as far as I could tell. We all knew he wasn't blind, but no one ever told him. He stood maybe four feet six inches. His dog was a terrier with an underbite. I said, "Did you see any heads back that way, Little Mickey?"

Mickey turned around. His dog didn't. Mickey held his hand up to shield rain and said, "There's a bunch of Cholly Lloyd's mannequins out in the street. I didn't see no heads. At first I thought I seen naked women passed out down on South Abney, but they was just Cholly's models."

I almost said, "Hey, Little Mickey, you want some free bourbon?" like that, like an idiot, like a cohort who kept another secret, but didn't. I said, "Okay," because I had an idea.

Cholly Lloyd knew mill workers, and wanted them to feel nothing but comfortable buying the clothes he offered. Cholly bought his mannequins from wherever people buy mannequins, and the first thing he did—before even covering them up in overalls and/or cotton dresses—was cut off their fingers down to the second joint.

Little Mickey said, "I'm glad tornadoes come in the way they do. From what I've heard, they don't hit the very bottom of the land."

I said, "Cholly Lloyd's mannequins are just lying around in the middle of the street? Is he there now looking at his problems?"

"I just kept tripping. I don't know. My dog couldn't get by, either. It's not like I could see what went on there, Warren Jr.," Little Mickey said.

I nodded like only a fourteen-year-old boy could do who'd drunk a half-pint of bourbon. I struggled my Winn-Dixie shopping cart past Mickey, splashed through puddles and potholes, and ran through my head the way professional wrestlers wrenched their opponents' necks.

Lookit: At the time I didn't know I'd marry a woman who would frame doilies, pillowcases, carved linen dinner napkins, and placemats, then put them up on every wall of the house as if they were paintings. I didn't know I'd go off to school and realize that maybe I didn't belong working in a town filled with cotton mills, or businessmen worried about digits, or for close relatives who believed that women's hair might fall off randomly. At the time I only focused on not getting caught doing about everything wrong I did.

I'm not sure what Cholly Lloyd's mannequins were made of—plaster of Paris or something—but with one good hard kick downward on the neck the heads snapped right off from the rest of their bodies. Just like my father's wig shop, Lloyd's clothing store had its windows blow right out, and the suction pulled out a good ten or twelve women, some completely naked and the others with their dresses up around their torsos. I didn't disturb the mannequins in any other way, and when one of them spun off like a tiddly wink or whatever when I stomped on her neck, I retrieved the rest of the body and placed it back on the asphalt in the same position I'd found her.

For some reason it seemed plausible to me that an insurance adjuster or meteorologist might want to take a tape measure and figure some things out.

I never found another styrofoam head or wig, but I returned to my daddy's store triumphant as a high-wire artist hailing from some sea level town going home. I said, "Check this out, Warren," to my father, which wasn't the smartest thing to do. People brought up in a cotton mill town didn't say their parents' first names, ever. Hell, if I'd've been in some kind of accident, knocked out with no identification on me outside of what my mother wrote in all my underwear, I'd've said "Mr. Mayhew" when I came to and answered some policeman's question about my father's full name and address.

My father said, "Son, did you sprain your ankles?"

"No," I said. I held on tight to the shopping cart handle. I said, "I found all these heads somewhere. They look like they got cut off from mannequins or something. Maybe you can act like they were yours all along, and pretend like there were wigs on them, and then tell the insurance agent you lost another thousand dollars, blah blah blah."

I actually said, "Blah blah blah," too. I shifted my weight from one leg to the other about four hundred times and knew I didn't make eye contact.

My father leaned his mop against a display for combs, brushes, and sheer stocking caps. He picked up one of the two bottles of Old Crow I'd brought him and untwisted the top. Me, I turned around and said something about how I once heard about baby torna-does that show up sometimes a day later after the big tornadoes. My father sniffed the bottle, then walked up to me and said, "Smell this."

I said, "I don't want to smell that stuff. It'll make

me sick to my stomach."

"Take a drink from it, Warren. I bet you can't make it bubble twice."

My father picked up one of the broken-off mannequin heads and poured a good two shots inside of it. He set the bottle down on a metal shelf uncapped, and then drank booze from the mannequin goblet he'd devised. My father said, "Aaah," like that, then, "There's nothing better than a woman's head, boy," but I'm not sure to this day if he meant it the way it sounded later on in my life.

I walked outside and sat down on the curb, trying to concentrate. Maybe I have reconstructed or reinvented my own history, but I'm almost certain that at that moment I knew I'd find a way out of a town where people didn't know that anything happened between the start of the Vietnam War until now unless they subscribed to national weekly magazines, seeing as the local paper ran nothing but human interest stories, and the local TV newscasters spent an entire hour talking about orphaned puppies, gardening techniques, the accomplishments of mentally handicapped children, and women's make-overs—except for once, that I remember.

"Damn you, Warren, that's you they're talking about, and believe-you-me they'll find out. Where's my business going to be once that happens?" my father yelled from his worn-out recliner. I was in my own bedroom reading that book by Fyodor Dostoyevsky, I swear. My parents wouldn't let me read Karl Marx, officially.

I yelled back, "What?"

My mother stood at my door by the time I looked that way. She said, "Please tell me that you're not a Satan-worshipper."

This was 1972, understand. I don't think the Satan-worship thing went on back then as much as it does today. And for that matter, in a hometown that just got nailed by a series of tornadoes, in a community run by three or four cotton mill-owning families, in a place where every Baptist preacher promised on Sunday mornings how God loved us more than He loved anyone, it didn't seem all that far-fetched from turning towards something else, really. I said, "I'm reading Dostoyevsky, not Nietzsche, Mom," even though I didn't know anything about Nietzsche. My French teacher told me that Nietzsche didn't believe in God, though. She was an idiot, I figured out later.

My father yelled for me to get in the den, and when I did he pointed at the television where some poor woman stood in the middle of the street, in front of Cholly Lloyd's clothes store. She said, "And now for a report on the telltale signs as to whether your teenage son or daughter believes in Satan is Dr. Owen Strang."

The woman in the street was the local reporter, Bea Marie Self—an ex-cheerleader who went on to college at some place like Clemson, didn't make the squad, then came back to her hometown to give us little news reports on upcoming fashion. Owen Strang was my pediatrician. Maybe he had some kind of training in abnormal psychology, I don't know.

Strang said, "A child who has no developed conscience or sense of self will start off by hurting family pets—let's say a dog, or a cat, or a little helpless goldfish—and then maybe venture out into the world of birds, squirrels, turtles, and frogs. If this behavior is not detected and squelched early on, we can only assume that he will later hurt humans and feel no remorse."

This guy droned on so much I was surprised his own children hadn't turned on him. He went off the air and the camera pointed back to Bea Marie Self, who wasn't prepared. She looked down at her heel to see if she stepped in something. My father said, "She's a nice girl. Her mother came in and bought a wig one time for a masquerade party."

Bea Marie looked back up and said, "Now, Dr. Strang told News 6 that decapitating mannequins certainly isn't in the same league as real men and women, but it may be a step between pets and people. If any of you parents out there have noticed noticeable changes in your son or daughter, Dr. Strang believes that you may want to seek professional help."

My mother said, "She comes from good family."

I wanted to say something about how I thought Bea Marie was an idiot, but didn't want my parents interpreting it as a noticeable change, and sending me away to some sanitarium. I said, "You never paid me that tip for the bourbon, Dad." He shook his head but couldn't help smiling. Then he handed me his empty glass and told me to make him another Tang and vodka.

These were the years before spy gadgetry, but I'd bet that if those little cameras parents now hide in teddy bears, potted plants, New Age sculptures, or fake mounted sailfish in order to spend entire evenings watching what the baby-sitter did all day, my mother and father would've installed them in my room. Every day until I went off to college I apologized to my father and tried to make him believe that I only wanted to help him out in regards to the insurance settlement. Somehow my father received no money whatsoever—and talked a bunch about karma, what-goes-around-comes-around, et cetera—because of some clause in his policy that mentioned how he wasn't covered against natural disasters. As it ended up, we would've been better off had I taken what wigs and styrofoam heads remained in his shop and hidden them around town, for he did have coverage against looters.

"What's that mark on your arm, Warren?" my mother said to me on a weekly basis.

"The dog jumped up and scratched me," I'd say, which was always the truth, unless "I had to go underneath Dad's shop and set some rat traps and scraped against the cement block," or "I accidentally stabbed myself with a protractor," or "We have a new girl in school with a hook-arm, I didn't know it, and I went to shake her hand," if that happened to be the truth. Not once did I even kid my parents and say something about burning coals, candles, Bunsen burners, or stray cats.

This is no lie: One time my mother asked me about a series of small marks on my neck and I said, "You told me it was a birthmark, Mom."

She said, "You were born without birthmarks, Warren. You came out just perfect. I don't know what happened between then and now."

Those ten bottles of Old Crow didn't last long in the spring house behind the Lutheran church, of course.

Listen, a few years after the tornado someone wanted my hometown to seem like a regular cosmopolitan place, so they tore down a vacant house two doors away from my father's store and built a three-tier parking garage. This was on a corner. What few business people and shoppers who needed to park would pass by the wig shop on Montague, take a right-hand turn into the garage, grab a ticket, and afterwards come down the ramps to exit on Waller Street where the attendant sat in a glass booth.

My father's business waned more than ever. The Savannah River nuclear plant didn't emit toxins like it used to, evidently.

Before I left town for good, each Saturday I walked from my father's store down to the parking garage and pushed the Push Here for Ticket button. I waited for the ticket and for the mechanical arm to raise and re-lower. Then I did it again. Usually it took about thirty minutes before the Lot Full light came on. I would sneak away and wonder what the attendant thought on the other side when his quiet shift ended.

From what I understand, people parked in front of Dad's store, and more women entered, and his business picked up. I know this: I never drove past Cholly Lloyd's clothing store again. My parents seemed to be relieved and much happier once I went out on my own, got an education, found a job outside of the textile industry, and settled down.

I visit regularly still, but we don't talk politics or religion. I don't mention to them, either, how to this day I can't take my wife on a vacation where we might walk past a distillery, or a wax museum, in any tourist town.

I Could've Told You if You Hadn't Asked

Desmond wanted to make a movie called *Chick-ens*. He wasn't sure if he had the imagination to pull it off, and he had no hope of grants or investors. The one thing he did possess was a beautiful but crazy wife, though I didn't know about her right off.

I had no money either, of course, but was getting some notoriety as a visionary what with the patch of gray hair on the back of my head that looked just like an eyeball, added to the fact that I'd predicted three Kentucky Derby winners in a row, the date of Black Monday, and Hurricane Hugo's strength, time and place of landing.

I could *see*, understand.

Desmond said, "Weldon, I know what I want to do will be a big seller. I just want you to give me the green light, guy. I call it *Chickens* for two reasons. First off there will be chickens in every scene—some-where strutting in the background, maybe. Second, I want to train the camera on people and ask them about what they fear more than anything else. I want a man to look into the camera and say, 'The gang violence around here is scaring me more than cor-nered rats.' Meanwhile he'll be eating a piece of fried chicken. *That's* subtext, man. I want to see a kid riding a homemade go-cart in circles around his parents' shack, going through a herd of chickens."

I said, "I don't think it's a herd. I think it's a clutch, or a brood. You might want to get that down

before trying to approach investors. It's a bed of
clams, and a cloud of gnats, and a sounder of boars.
It's a troop of monkeys and a knot of toads—that's
my favorite, a *knot* of toads." I'd memorized the
World Almanac, 'cause it had this kind of information.

Desmond stood there in the small kitchen of my
small cabin. I drank Old Crow mixed with ginger ale
and milk thistle to help replenish my liver. I'd been
sitting there almost non-stop—not always drinking,
of course—since getting fired from my job a year
earlier at Coca-Cola in Atlanta. I had worked in an
advisory and public relations capacity, but I'd been on
a downward run with the higher-ups ever since I said
publicly that the new Coke they wanted to market
wouldn't work whatsoever.

Desmond said, "You know I'm not as smart as
some people think I am. I'll admit that. You know my
wife wants to leave me because she has fulfillment
issues. She says I'm not performing to what she saw
as my capacity when we married."

I said, "You're going to have to give me a minute
to think this one out. It might take me some time to
puzzle out what Hollywood wants, and what the
people want."

Desmond said, "I need some time to write out the
script anyway."

He wore a pair of khakis that didn't quite fit anymore. They hung down low, and his stomach stuck
out like a silhouette of Stone Mountain down in
Georgia. Desmond and his nutty wife moved from
New York down to Christ Almighty, North Carolina,
about the same time I made enough money to move
up and buy a summer cabin, long before I understood
that I might have to move there for good. Desmond
thought he'd absorb some of the South for the best-
selling novel he planned to write, but the South absorbed him.

Desmond pulled out the chair across from me and
sat down. I said, "There's a job down in Tryon with
First Realty. They're looking for someone to put up
For Sale signs. I think they pay ten bucks to put up a
sign, and five for pulling it down once the house is

sold. Here's what you do—get the job. Put up the signs. At night drive around and knock the signs down. They'll ask you to put the signs back up and you'll get paid twice. Let's say you only have ten signs a week. That's only $100 a week. But if you keep knocking them down, you could make fifty bucks more. Plus you get the five dollars for what sells." I mention this conversation to show that, contrary to his subsequent claims, I told him all these scams *before* I ever laid eyes on his wife.

Desmond said, "I want to make movies. Films, dude. I've given up writing novels about upper-middle-class people trying to find out about themselves in new and exciting ways."

I got up and made another drink without as much milk thistle because I felt dangerous. I said, "After you make the money by peckering around with real estate agents, go put down money on a lush apartment. You put down one month's rent and the security deposit. Pay in cash. Lie about your name. Then place a want ad in the papers for the apartment for about half what you pay."

Desmond said, "Weldon. I don't want to go to jail."

"You ain't going to jail, man," I said. "You're a film maker. How many film makers are in jail, outside of that guy who can't come back to America for what he did with an underage female?"

Desmond held his head funny. I told him to get some nice furniture, tell prospective renters that he'd gotten a one-year job somewhere and wanted to keep the apartment. I told him to get a post office box and a telephone his wife wouldn't know about.

Desmond said, "Five people a day come in for one month. I show them the apartment, say it's furnished, and take their money?"

I said, "Ask for cash. Say you don't believe in checks. Give them receipts. In no time you got enough money to make your movie." Before Desmond could think about it, I said, "Three hundred dollars for the first month, $300 for the security— that's $600. Six hundred times 150 people. That's

$90,000. Hell, rent out three or four apartments and you can go beyond documentary-style black-and-whites. Goddamn, boy, I see a major motion picture in your future."

Desmond said, "My wife's not a patient woman, Weldon. This has to happen fast."

I said, "Go rob a bank. Rob a bank, then make your movie. I wouldn't, but you might."

Desmond shook his head. He pulled his khakis up, then combed his hand through where he wanted more hair. Outside, a hawk circled above Lake Christ Almighty. I tried to think about people in a theater, watching a movie with chickens in every frame, but couldn't.

I found Desmond's wife dumping ice deliberately, a ritual I'd heard about but taken for myth. Desmond's wife went in the back door to their added-on house, and brought back one of those styrofoam chests for transporting good meats or vital organs. She stepped softly. She was wearing padded bedroom slippers. I didn't speak, because what she was doing looked a lot like what I imagined ancient Asian religious folks did during their somber ceremonies, or how a talented seer might act outside in times of rare planetary alignments. Desmond's wife sprayed Num-Zit first-aid medicine between her ice mounds.

"Are your soles soft rubber?" she asked with her back turned. I swear to God this is true. What I'm saying is, this woman was both cosmological and ontological somehow. She may have been teleological, too, but I don't remember all my metaphysics from college.

I said, "I just wanted to come and see if Desmond was doing OK. I just wanted to see what he's working on these days." I wasn't sure if he'd told his wife about *Chickens*. I didn't want to give any secrets away in case he kept plans to himself. It's a male code.

Desmond's wife stood there holding the styrofoam. She wore a thin cotton print skirt that let light flow through—her upper thighs could've been used as sturdy, solid thin masts, is what I'm saying—and a T-shirt that read Vote Your Uterus. It kind of gave me the creeps, but I swear I couldn't keep my eyes off it. She had big knockers. Desmond's wife said, "The earth is our mother. Walk softly. I'm about to plant a garden, and I don't want my mother to hurt whatsoever. I'm numbing her skin before I dig. I'm numbing the dirt before I dig or hoe or scrape."

I couldn't say anything except, "Shew—I don't want to hurt the earth none. I wouldn't also want to disturb a grist of bees or a down of hares." What the hell.

Desmond's wife said, "You didn't major in geology did you? I hope you didn't major in geology."

I about told her I never went to college. I said, "No. I majored in philosophy in undergraduate school. Then I went on to law school and quit before the year was over. I never was good at the sciences, really."

"Geologists become miners. Miners end up drilling holes in the earth. You wouldn't go to a dentist and have him drill into your teeth without any kind of pain killer would you?"

I said, "Tell Desmond I came by and I'll try to get in touch with him later." I started to walk away, back around the cold shallow lake to my little cabin. I kept thinking how men down here pride themselves on not coon dogging what's already been treed. We don't actively pursue a married man's wife, is what I'm saying. We kill the husband more often than not, or at least get him in a situation that involves a long prison sentence. Thinking about it almost made me have a Pentecostal fit, all thick-tongued and spastic.

"You ever been to a proctologist?" Desmond's wife asked me. She didn't seem to squint as much as she seemed to want to cry, or pass two stones the size of a bad carpenter's thumbs.

I said, "I just sit in my room and think, ma'am. I work as a freelance consultant these days when admen can't come up with ideas and don't want to lose their jobs. Please don't judge me or anything, please."

Desmond's wife said, "My husband went down the mountain to do some work. He won't be back until way past ten or eleven tonight."

This was a Sunday. Realty offices were closed. I knew what Desmond was doing. I laughed and said, "Hey, do you cover your land in sheets of plastic when it hails?"

Desmond's wife took out a little memo pad note-book from the elastic band in her skirt, and wrote down something. She smiled, and raised her eye-brows. She looked like God let her down on a hand-made sunbeam.

I didn't understand until later that maybe women from up North kept track of when their husbands returned. Maybe I'd gotten too caught up in my own ways to realize Desmond's wife was sending me a signal.

I left Desmond's wife and went home until the sun went down. Then I made my way backwards towards every sign I'd seen lately from First Realty, knowing he'd be nearby in stocking cap and black gloves, sweating from the humidity. I found him hidden halfway down in a carport adjacent to the sort of solid cedar-shake shingle house admired and purchased by people who have a thing for armadillos and alluvial outcroppings.

I said, "Desmond! Get out of there, man, it's me!"

Desmond shimmied goofily, holding his hand up against my pick-up's beam. He said, "Weldon, you scared the shit out of me."

I said, "I meant to. Your wife said you wouldn't be back until late, so I surmised that you got a job doing what I said."

"Well," Desmond said. "I got to do what I got to do in order to do what I want to do, you know."

I said, "Uh-huh."

We shook hands. He'd already thrown down the For Sale sign a good twenty feet from where he had planted it earlier.

Desmond said, "You didn't tell me to wear different-sized shoes when I did this. But I'm wearing different-sized shoes. I went down to a Salvation Army place in Spartanburg and bought three pairs of boots ranging two to four sizes too big than what I wear. I wear a normal ten. I figure no one would be able to trace it back to me—unless they open the woodbin where I keep them during the day."

I said, "There are no cops in Christ Almighty, Desmond. I think you're pretty safe."

He said, "You didn't tell Fiona where you thought I might be, did you?"

I thought, *Fiona*. I had never met a woman named Fiona, but it seemed like a Fiona would be either the kind of woman who'd numb the earth before digging into it or the kind who welcomed strays. I said, "When she told me you wouldn't be back until ten or eleven tonight I told her you probably drove all the way to Charlotte looking for a strip joint. Now don't go committing suicide with that post hole digger."

He said, "OK."

"It's a joke," I said. "I didn't tell her anything, you idiot."

"You don't know my wife, Weldon," he said. "I'm not real proud of it, but I have a girlfriend back in New York. I tell my wife I'm going back to deal with an agent or editor. Actually I lost both my agent and my editor. It's a long story that involves a favorite uncle and his cousin's wife's daughter."

Desmond laughed. I tried not to make eye contact and found myself staring at his chin more than anything else. I said, "That's OK," though I didn't think it was. Listen, I took those marriage vows seriously— even my ex-wife would have to back me up on that one.

We stood while two jets flew overhead, almost side by side. In the brush beside this house a doe rambled, bedding down. I thought about my ex-wife in my ex-city, living not so far from my ex-job. I handed Desmond a beer out of the bed of my truck and said, "There are no chickens living nearby. What're you going to do about that?"

"When I wrote novels I didn't care about truth," he said. "I published a novel about Vietnam and the women's lingerie industry. To be honest, I didn't know squat about either. I'm from Brooklyn. All you need to know applies to both subjects—camouflage only works for so long."

I did not say how it was the same thing in advertising. I didn't say anything because it looked like we were bonding in the dark, and that scared me. I said, "Chickens."

He said, "I put ads in some magazines up north for the apartment. People come down here in the winter, you know. I even said it was a condo."

It would've been a good time to tell Desmond that I was only joking, that I made everything up about how he could make money. But his wife worried that the earth hurt, and I worried that she hurt, too. That's all I could think about there in the dark with one For Sale sign down and another fifty or so scattered around the mountain. No comet, or shooting star, or UFO showed itself. No Dodge Dart skidded around the curve carrying a trunkload of moonshine. I did not smell marijuana burning anywhere, though I felt hungry and responsible, as always.

"Desmond," I said. "Desmond, Desmond, Desmond. I may have made a mistake by telling you how to make money to support a movie. Don't you have any family that believes in you?"

I turned the lights off in my truck and left the engine running. I barely saw him, is what I'm saying. Desmond said, "My dad's dead and my mother thinks I'm still going to write the great fucking American novel. I can't let her down." He shuffled a foot in sparse gravel and said, "I don't have any brothers or sisters, and I wasn't that popular growing up."

I didn't ask if Fiona had anyone. I kind of knew. I said, "Fiona numbed the earth so she wouldn't hurt it any when she planted a garden, or something. Have you thought about keeping the camera turned on her? I don't want to make any judgment about you and yours, but I bet a documentary about your wife would be interesting. Hell, all you'd have to do is buy some security cameras and set them up."

Desmond took a draw from his beer and threw it back into the bed of my truck. He said, "That might be an idea, *paisan*."

I said, "When's the last time you saw a movie about a person who did things a whole lot differently than anyone else?"

"I don't remember offhand," Desmond said. "I could've told you if you hadn't asked."

With that response I knew Desmond needed to go back up north. No one in his or her right mind below the Mason-Dixon line answered questions with "I could've told you if you hadn't asked." It didn't even make sense. If it did, people would just walk around aimlessly spouting out answers like, "Carson City is the capital, not Las Vegas or Reno!" or "Robert Duvall played Boo Radley!" or "Jupiter's equatorial diameter is 88,000 miles," or "Tonga's chief crops are coconut products, bananas, and vanilla."

I said, "Goddamn, if you got such a hard-on for chickens, maybe you can buy a couple roosters and keep them on your property so they'll show up in some scenes with Fiona."

I did not, of course, mean this in an odd poker-night, jokey way. Desmond took off his watch cap, wiped his forehead, and laughed without thinking about how it might be heard all up and down the mountain, through two valleys, past his job at the real estate agent's office, and into whatever apartment he rented there at the foot of Mount Christ Almighty on the Pacolet River "Where Retirees Can Enjoy the Splendor of Country Mountain Living."

I do not know the cost of spy gadgetry, and didn't ask Desmond how many signs he set up, knocked down, and re-set over a two-month period. He bought his chickens first, over the complaints of the home association, and later set up cameras one at a time when Fiona drove down the mountain for ice, Bactine, gauze, Neosporin, and whatever else she used to help heal the mother on which we live.

I know I found myself looking across a quadrant of lake water too often. I used binoculars, hoping to see Fiona bent over in a less-than-modest dress. I thought about how my wife was long gone.

The first time I met Fiona she knew I was watching her numb the soil, so I should have known she could feel me watching her two hundred yards away. One morning she knocked on my door and I answered. When she said, "You want a telescope?" I could only hope that I heard wrong.

"Hey, Fiona. Come on in for some coffee," I said.

She said, "Is it one of those flavored coffees? You know those flavored coffees have chemicals in them that they don't advertise on the box."

I said, "It's regular coffee. I have some bread, too. I was just about to have breakfast. Come on in."

She stood there wearing the only skirt I'd ever seen her wear, the one that sunlight ravished without much effort. Fiona said, "Weldon, right?"

I said, "Uh-huh."

She said, "I know when you're watching me, Weldon. You aren't doing anything weird up here, are you?"

I said, "I'll confess that I watch you. I've never seen anyone care about blemishes so much. I apologize, and I'll quit, but I promise I'm not doing anything perverted. I've had a wife and I've had girlfriends. Not at the same time, either—I took a course in ethics one time in college."

That wasn't true. I mean, I had not taken a course in ethics, which I figured gave me the right to tell a lie. Fiona said, "Did you use any preservatives in your bread?"

I told her I washed my hands between each knead.

When we fucked daily for the next six weeks we did so slowly. Fiona wasn't sure about my cabin's pilings—whether or not they were planted loosely— or whether our rhythm might tamp down into her mother like the misstroke of a blunt-ended tooth

brush that jabs your gums. I did not her tell her
about her husband's uncle's cousin's daughter. I did
not the break male code in that way. And there was
no love between Fiona and me, at least that first
week: We only whispered about the earth moving,
often.

But I said more than once in her ear, "Where were
you when I thought I should get married?"

"Probably getting married. Or in Santa Fe learning
massage therapy," Fiona said to me more often than
not.

Desmond came over finally in mid-summer. I felt
uncomfortable, of course. We hadn't spoken since I
told him to scrap *Chickens*. Desmond said, "Weld-on,
I've been thinking. I don't want to be nosy, but how
do you live? You don't work in advertising anymore,
do you, Weld-on? You don't have a home office upstairs so you can just fax what you're thinking, do you
Weld-on?"

Desmond seemed to have something to say.

I said, "I saved money well and invested OK. I
work as a consultant sometimes but don't seek it.
I don't like to brag or anything, but people in the
industry know me, and when they're out of ideas they
get in touch and offer me money. An adman without
an idea is an ex-adman in about a 30-second spot."

Desmond said, "Huh."

I said, "I thought you'd be wearing a beret by now.
How's it going?"

"Oh, I'm *set*, amigo," he said. I poured bourbon.
"I ain't got a story line or anything but figure I can do
it through editing. Are you sure this'll work out?"
Desmond didn't sit down when I shoved the chair out
for him.

I couldn't lie. I said, "Well. Maybe your wife's not
as quirky as I thought."

"So you're saying Fiona's not odd enough to star
in my film, is that what you're saying? You saying my
wife's too *average* to care about? I don't think you
know what you mean, Weldon."

Desmond had a different edge to him. He bowed up on me good. People in the South sometimes think Northerners display a certain curtness, a certain broad and blatant cruelty towards other human beings. It's a misconception that thrives with others— such as how dead black snakes on fence posts end droughts or crossing a downhill stream will stop a specter. People from the Northeast are kind, really. Unlike me—and the people I know—they don't constantly scheme at ways to kill friends, acquaintances, and relatives.

I said, "I'm saying I don't know what I'm saying."

Desmond held his fists at his sides. In this short time I'd already considered throwing him off my porch headfirst, taking the fire poker to his temple, even rigging a clipped and frayed electrical wire from an outlet into my toilet so when he peed out his bourbon it'd shock him hard. When I stuck up one index finger and shook it like a scolding mother from a fifties movie, Desmond evidently thought I foreplayed a shot to his nose. He decked me quick, then. He said, "I know about you fucking Fiona, Weld-on. I got movies and I got a lawyer."

I've realized that the more isolated a person attempts to be, the more people know about him. I'm sure everyone on Mount Christ Almighty, and the valley towns of Tryon and Columbus, even smaller Lynn and Green Creek, knew that I had a scalp condition that required dandruff shampoo. Or that I had the occasional bout with athlete's foot when I worked in scawmy conditions, or that I had hemorrhoids from worrying too much about my goddamn feet. People knew these things because I could do my grocery shopping at one place only—a family-owned store down the mountain called Powell's.

When this buzz-cut kid handed me a subpoena to show up at Fiona and Desmond's divorce proceeding he held a handkerchief to his mouth. I said, "Have you got a bad cold or something? I took a bath this morning."

"I don't want to get the tuberculosis," he said.

"I ain't got TB."

"Well, you had to go down to the doctor last week, and you haven't bought any cigarettes since, and you had a coughing fit down at the Waffle House," the kid said.

"Oh. Oh, yeah. It's not tuberculosis, man," I said. "It's rabies." I took two quick steps his way so he jumped clean off the porch, eight feet off the ground.

I'd gone to the doctor to get some shots, because I'd been hired to check out the chances of a Disney project in Kuwait. I told them to save their money, but they didn't. That Gulf War thing took place soon thereafter. There you go.

I lied in front of the judge and jury, in front of the packed house at the Polk County courthouse, in front of Fiona, Desmond, and their respective lawyers. I said, "No sir, I never had sex with her in my house. It's true she came over as the films indicate." Then I said, "On more than one occasion Fiona came over looking for Bactine, Neosporin, and gauze." I made it sound like Desmond beat her or something, but I didn't care.

Desmond had the brains to point one of his little cameras towards my front porch. The jury saw something like forty-two clips of Fiona walking in my front door, all but one of me hugging her there. When Desmond took the stand he swore I'd told him about my scams just so I could lure his wife over my way. He'd put his hand on the Bible and everything, and looked the jury straight. Obviously they believed him. Luckily, no chicken followed Fiona over or we might have been sentenced to the electric chair. This was the South.

Of course she lost everything. Juries from the mountains of western North Carolina don't care about mental cruelty or impotence or abuse. It's as if "Stand By Your Man" is piped into the chambers.

The prosecutor asked me, "Do you know what kind of person you are, breaking up a marriage?" I sat silent. "You're nothing but a coward, lying like this. Do you know the meaning of coward?"

I tried not to shake. I didn't look up or down, or sideways back and forth haphazardly, like an animal confused by rain.

I didn't mention to Desmond's lawyer how the mountains of North Carolina are filled with garnets and rubies and emeralds and mica. I didn't say how one day when Fiona came over she made me lie naked in the sun, and placed semi-precious gems on what she understood to be pressure points on my body.

I understood, too. I'm talking sundial—she put a rock right on the end of my pecker. Fiona said, "I'm trying to learn the proper and beneficial uses of magnets, but I don't feel sure about myself yet."

In the distance we heard Desmond's roosters crow. Fiona put rocks on herself, and we both fell asleep. I got a sunburn, and when I woke up it looked like someone had written tiny O's on my body. I'd never felt better in my life—when Fiona rolled over on me our white marks fit like pistons, I swear. Let me say right now that it was at this point that I knew I loved Fiona, and could work as the conductor on her trainload of neuroses. Call it luck or predilection on her part, but those stones made me feel different about myself and the rest of the world, and the way things would end up in the future.

The prosecutor said, "Boy, I believe you got some Sherman in you, what with the way you burned a marriage with a perfect foundation." He pointed over at Desmond and said, "What else could you have done to this poor man?"

Years later on, reading about how *Chickens* won those independent-film competitions, I had all kinds of reactions, most of which involved duct tape, a hard-backed simple chair, a pistol butt, and a smile. I read that in France the movie was called *Les Poulets*, of course, and audiences considered it some kind of classic. In Holland or Denmark the film went by plain *Peep-peep*. Because Desmond won the divorce, he also got the house and half of Fiona's worth, enabling him to back himself on his own project. Fiona came from a wealthy family, too. What I'm saying is, I damn near forgot that women named Fiona either numbed the ground when they walked, or took in strays, or had a trust fund the size of influenza.

We live quietly these days and we compromise. Sometimes Fiona circles that gray patch on the back of my head as if she were mixing a drink with her finger. She says I'll come up with a vision for us both. I don't make fun of her when she goes outside at night and cries with the stars and moon. And unlike most people, I'm now allowed to stomp on this earth.

About the Authors

Rosa Shand

Rosa Shand was raised in Columbia, South Carolina, but then headed off to Virginia (Randolph-Macon), Uganda, New York, and Texas (the University at Austin). She's published over twenty-five stories in such journals as *The Southern Review*, *The South Carolina Review*, *The Virginia Quarterly Review*, *Shenandoah*, and *The Massachusetts Review*. She has won the Katherine Anne Porter Prize, been the South Carolina Fellow in Fiction, had readings at the Library of Congress and on National Public Radio, won the South Carolina Fiction Project several times, and held fellowships from the MacDowell Colony, Yaddo, and the Virginia Center for the Creative Arts.

Three manuscripts of hers are ready to be published somewhere someday—a linked collection of African stories (one of two runners-up in the national Associated Writing Programs contest), a collection of Southern stories, and a novel.

Thirteen years ago, when she settled in Spartanburg and heard that the new South Carolina Academy of Authors had, in their first year, honored Mary Boykin Chesnut, Dubose Heyward, and Julia Peterkin, she had an eerie feeling she'd come home. Her mother was Mary Boykin Heyward, a relative of the first two; and she was teaching at Converse College, the alma mater of Peterkin, South Carolina's only winner of the Pulitzer Prize.

Scott Gould

Born near a swamp in Kingstree, South Carolina. Soon after began steady movement northward. Lexington. Spartanburg. Greenville. Progress ultimately stopped by Blue Ridge Mountains. Attended Wofford College. (Warm memories.) Attended graduate school at the University of South Carolina. (Basic memories.) Published stories in *Kenyon Review*, *Kansas Review*, *Carolina Quarterly*, *Black Warrior Review*, *Crescent Review*, *New Stories from the South*, and many other literary hideaways.

Published chapbook of poems, *Jukebox Love*. Has won awards for fiction, poetry, screenwriting, and teaching: South Carolina Arts Literary Fellowship, South Carolina Academy of Authors Fellowship—things of that ilk.

Used to teach at Greenville's Fine Arts Center and South Carolina's Governor's School for the Arts. Used to want to be the next Larry Bird. Used to have good knees. Currently has job as writer and associate creative director at Phillips & Goot in Greenville. Loves fly fishing. Goes occasionally. Loves kids. Has two. Loves wife. Has one. Tolerates pets. Has too many.

DENO TRAKAS

Deno Trakas has a hundred-year connection to Spartanburg, South Carolina: his paternal grandfather was a founder of the Greek community there at the turn of the century; both his parents were raised there; and he has lived there with his family for eighteen years. He teaches English and coaches tennis at Wofford College, a block away from his grandmother's house, which is the setting for "The Philosopher's Landlord," although the rest of the story is a figment of his imagination.

His poetry and fiction have been published in more than two dozen publications, including *Denver Quarterly*, *The Louisville Review* and *The Oxford American*. He is working on a second chapbook of poems, *Human and Puny* (forthcoming from Holocene Press), and a novel, *After Paris* (which is set in Spartanburg in the twenties and thirties), and he will keep writing without hope and without despair, and occasionally sending out his work, and occasionally publishing, until his friend John Lane makes him famous, which he has promised to do.

GEORGE SINGLETON

George Singleton grew up in Greenwood, South Carolina, and was educated at Furman University and the University of North Carolina at Greensboro. He has stood at the front of a number of classrooms while students, aged fifteen to eighty-five, stared at him. In the summers, Singleton grows a variety of hot peppers in his garden, then gives them away. He roams flea markets whenever possible, in search of ashtrays and stories. Sometimes he finds ashtrays.

He lives outside Dacusville, South Carolina, or on top of Skyuka Mountain, North Carolina, with clay artist Glenda Guion and their eight dogs and one cat. When he's not picking peppers, or scouring the flea market, or writing, or standing near a chalkboard, he pretty much drives around aimlessly taking dogs for rides. On occasion, the cat gets to go.

Singleton has published about fifty stories that have appeared in *New Stories from the South—The Year's Best* (1994 and 1998), *Playboy*, *Writers Harvest 2*, *The Georgia Review*, *Shenandoah*, *Fiction International*, *American Literary Review*, *Greensboro Review*, *Cimarron*, *The Chariton Review*, *Denver Quarterly*, *South Carolina Review*, and elsewhere.

Publication of *New Southern Harmonies* has been made possible by the generous contributions of the following:

THE ARTS PARTNERSHIP OF GREATER SPARTANBURG

Mr. and Mrs. Stan Baker
Dr. and Mrs. Jim Bradof
Ms. Marshall Chapman
Mr. and Mrs. John Cobb
Converse College
Mr. and Mrs. Arthur Cleveland
The Rev. Beth Ely
Mr. and Mrs. Roger Habisreutinger
Mr. Winston Hardegree
Ms. Agnes Harris
Intermedia
Mr. and Mrs. E. Lewis Miller
McMillan Smith & Partners
Olencki Graphics, inc.
Phillips & Goot
Mr. and Mrs. Dwight Patterson
Mr. and Mrs. Robert V. Pinson
Ms. Betsy Wakefield Teter
Wofford College
Mrs. Cynthia Wood

Publication of this book is funded in part by the Arts Partnership of Greater Spartanburg and its donors, the County and City of Spartanburg, and the South Carolina Arts Commission which receives support from the National Endowment for the Arts.

All proceeds from the sale of this book go to the Hub City Writers Project Fund of the Spartanburg County Foundation, which funds our organization.

The Hub City Writers Project is a non-profit organization whose mission is to foster a sense of community through the literary arts. We do this by publishing books from and about our community; encouraging, mentoring, and advancing the careers of local writers; and seeking to make Spartanburg a center for the literary arts.

Our metaphor of organization purposely looks backward to the nineteenth century when Spartanburg was known as the "hub city," a place where railroads converged and departed.

As we approach the twenty-first century, Spartanburg is fast becoming a literary hub of South Carolina with an active and nationally celebrated core group of poets, fiction writers, and essayists. We celebrate these writers—and the ones yet born—as one of our community's greatest assets. William R. Ferris, former director of the Center for the Study of Southern Cultures, says of the emerging South, "Our culture is our greatest resource. We can shape an economic base . . . And it won't be an investment that will disappear."

Holocene 1998

Not only the present geologic epoch, but a micropublisher in upstate South Carolina. We feature limited editions of poetry, broadsides, travel journals, and intelligent prose, including The Hub City Writers Project series.

Yip-A Cowboy's Howl • David Romtvedt
Usumacinta River Journey • John Lane, editor
To See A World • John Harrington
Carvings on a Prayer Tree • Jim Peterson
The Questions of Postmodernism • David Lehman
Weed Time • John Lane
The Stars of Canaan • Rucht Lilavivat
Juke Box Love • Scott Gould

Vale of Academe • Stephen Sandy
An Afternoon with K • Jim Peterson
Hub City Anthology • John Lane & Betsy Teter, editors
Hub City Music Makers • Peter Cooper
Hub City Christmas • John Lane & Betsy Teter, editors
Long Division • Janet Wondra
Chromata • D. E. Steward
The Joshua Requiem • Travis Wheeler

Colophon

New Southern Harmonies was conceived and designed utilizing Adobe® PageMaker® 6.5 on a "still limping" Power Macintosh® 7100/80 using MacOS 7.5, packing semi-quad drives (totaling 4.3 gigs of possible storage, 1 gig still, alas, inaccessible, but in a box on the floor *near* the computer), 132 meg of ram, the ever faithful HP ScanJet IIcx®, an indispensable Polariod Sprint-Scan 35 Plus®, and a newly acquired iomega® zip™ drive and its bigger brother the 1GB jaz™ drive in a first edition of 2000 soft-bound and a limited edition of 125 case-bound copies. The display typeface is the recently released Pablo. The body typeface family is ITC Leawood®. The seasoned book designer (and his weary helpers) found creative inspiration and a safe harbor with OBAN®, the 'Little Bay of Caves,' along the shores of Argyll, Scotland.